Lotus
and
Other Tales of Medieval Japan

Lotus
and
Other Tales
of
Medieval Japan

Takeshi Umehara
translated by Paul McCarthy

CHARLES E. TUTTLE COMPANY
Rutland, Vermont & Tokyo, Japan

Illustrations by Shin Fujihira

Originally published as *Chusei Shosetsu-shu*, Shinchosha, 1993

Visit Tuttle Web on the Internet at:
http://www.tuttle.co.jp/~tuttle/

Published by the Charles E. Tuttle Company, Inc.
of Rutland, Vermont & Tokyo, Japan
with editorial offices at
2-6 Suido 1-chome, Bunkyo-ku, Tokyo 112

© 1996 by Charles E. Tuttle Publishing Co., Inc.

All rights reserved

LCC Card No. 96-61006
ISBN 0-8048-2062-7 (hardback)
ISBN 0-8048-2098-8 (paperback)

First edition, 1996

Printed in Japan

Contents

Acknowledgments • 7

Preface • 9

Heads • 15

Haseo's Love • 35

The Nun Oyō • 55

A Tale of Luck and Riches • 75

Lazybones Tarō • 97

Lotus • 119

How the Gods Came to Kumano • 145

Sanshō Dayū • 171

Acknowledgments

This translation is dedicated to the memory of the late Professor Edward Copeland of the University of Minnesota, a man of the broadest culture and a dedicated teacher-scholar under whom I first had the privilege of studying Japanese literature as an undergraduate; and to Professor Amy Matsumoto, formerly of the University of Minnesota, a sensitive poet and skillful mentor to whom I have been indebted over the years as teacher, colleague, and friend. Finally, I want to thank Mr. Donald Richie of Tokyo and Ms. Sachiko Usui of the International Center for Research in Japanese Studies in Kyoto, without whose kind help and encouragement this translation would not have been possible.

—The Translator

Preface

Takeshi Umehara (b. 1925) is a distinguished Japanese scholar, administrator, and writer who began with the study of Western philosophy at Kyoto University (which has a strong tradition of philosophical studies, both Western and Eastern) but found himself gradually drawn more and more toward research in early Japanese history, religious thought, and literature. He has written extensively and provocatively about especially enigmatic aspects of Japan's past: *Kakusareta jūjika* ("The Hidden Cross: A Study of the Hōryū-ji," 1972) deals with the mysterious relation between this hugely important religious institution and cultural monument from the seventh century and the figure of its princely patron, Shōtoku Taishi, himself a religious, political, and cultural icon through the ages. *Minasoko no uta* ("Songs from the Depths: A Study of Kakinomoto-no-Hitomaro," 1973) examines the life and work of the most brilliaht poet of the earliest classical poetic anthology, the *Man'yōshū*. Other works have probed the nature of the struggle between the

Jomon and Yayoi cultures in prehistoric and protohistoric Japan (*Nihon bōken*, "The Japan Adventure," 1988–89); or the nature of Japanese views on the afterlife, which Umehara believes to be both characteristic and formative of the culture (*Jigoku no shisō*, "The Idea of Hell," 1967; and *Nihonjin no anoyo-kan*, "Japanese Views on the Next World," 1989). He is currently at work on a full-scale biography of the medieval Buddhist reformer and saint Hōnen and the founding of the Pure Land pietist movement.

Over the past few years, Umehara has begun a "second career" as a creative writer. First there was a series of plays: *Yamato-takeru* (1988), *Gilgamesh* (1988), and *Oguri Hangan* (1991), dramatic depictions of the careers of great cultural heroes of ancient Japan, Sumeria, and medieval Japan, respectively. *Yamato-takeru* and *Oguri Hangan* were performed as new-style "Super Kabuki" by Ichikawa Ennosuke and his troupe, enjoying long runs and popular acclaim. Now Umehara has attempted a new genre, the tale, which is intimately connected with his scholarly interest in medieval Buddhist Japan. He seems to be seeking to present a more personal vision of Japanese culture and, indeed, of human life through this non-dramatic, more private and reflective literary form. Each of the pieces in *Eight Tales of Medieval Japan* is based upon a medieval model ("medieval" here covering a very broad time-span, from roughly the twelfth through the sixteenth centuries). The original stories are of various types including *setsuwa*, *otogi-zōshi*, and *sekkyō-bushi*. The precise boundaries of these genres are rather difficult to delimit, but they are in general fictional (or fictionalized) stories combining entertainment (comic, erotic, adventurous, bizarre) with moral-religious instruction. They were popular art forms characteristic of the Middle Ages, as more aristocratic, romantic-aesthetic works like *The Tale of Genji* were of the earlier Court-centered culture. As such, their literary effects are usually quite direct, requiring relatively little learning for their appreciation. The world they depict is full of religious, supernaturalist elements—ghosts appear, oracles are consulted, miracles are performed; and popular Buddhist ideas like the workings of karma through a chain of lifetimes, the compassionate concern of buddhas and bodhisattvas for their devotees, and the perils of folly, anger, and greed form an essential part of the world-picture that underlies these stories. (Some of the original collections have been translated into English, in whole or in part: see, for example, Marian Ury's *Tales of Times Now Past* and D. E. Mills' *A Collection of Tales from Uji*, as well as studies and translations of Muromachi period *otogi-zōshi* by Barbara Ruch, Margaret H. Childs, and several other scholars.

Umehara has taken these tales and "fleshed them out" in his own way. The Buddhist (or Shintō, or folk-religious) elements are preserved, though often with touches of irony. The purely entertaining features tend to be expanded and elaborated in a highly individual manner. One thinks, for example, of the literary fun that is had with the "artful farting" at the center of "A Tale of Luck and Riches": the mock-learned references to Zeami's theories of Noh performance, the moral revelations of vanity and covetousness occasioned by rivalry over the new "wind-instrument," etc. If many of the elements of the original have been preserved (folk-religion, didacticism, humorous scatology), other aspects seem new: sympathy for the plight of the defeated Fukutomi almost balances admiration for the successful Takamuku and the wiley wife who is responsible for his rise. (And yet we last glimpse Takamuku, in a final reversal of fortune, literally caught in the jaws of his defeated rival's terrifying wife.) Two characteristic types of the medieval period are the monk and the soldier. They are as representative of the culture of the Middle Ages as the courtier and court-lady are of the Heian period or the townsman of Edo. There had always been military men, of course, but now they dominated political and social life in a new, more direct way. Buddhism too had long been an important feature of Japanese life; but during the Kamakura period, the originally foreign faith was fully naturalized, with new sects springing up that appealed to a far broader spectrum of people than the earlier, more scholastic and elitist schools had done. One of the stories in this collection, "Lotus," is an especially good example of the trends of the new age, for its hero is both a soldier and a monk, an actual historical figure who appears in, for example, the *Life of Hōnen* in forty-eight fascicles, on parts of which this story is based. As the valiant warrior Kumagai Jirō Naozane, he features in the epic military chronicle *The Tale of the Heike*. As the repentant priest Rensei-bō, he appears in the Noh play *Atsumori*, calming the angry ghost of the youth he killed in battle many years before. In Umehara's story, he is a monk intent above all on salvation in the form of rebirth in Amida Buddha's Pure Land, attainable through faith and repetition of the Holy Name. But as a warrior, he had always been the one to lead the charge on the enemy camp; and now, as a Pure Land devotee, he wanted only the highest, most difficult "grade" of rebirth. And so we have a tale of double conversion: from proud, fierce warrior to earnest, but still quite arrogant, believer; and from that to a truly humble man of faith, now at last capable of the highest form of salvation. The large religious concern is typical of much of Umehara's writing, as is the accompanying comic realism of detail, which might seem to undercut it but in fact does not. Indeed, one key to Umehara's literature seems to me to be the successful harmonizing of apparent opposites: of seriousness with comedy, often of a rather broad sort; of Buddhist compassion with unembarrassed accounts of cruelty;

of sensitivity to the "religion of beauty" and delight in frankly scatological detail. Almost all of the tales are full of these apparent contradictions—one thinks of the terrible cruelty and crassness of Sanshō Dayū's son Saburō toward the innocent children set against the revelation of his love for his reprobate father. And though, unlike Mori Ōgai in his early-modern version of the story, Umehara refuses to allow the father's head to stay on his shoulders, he does assure us that even this villain can be saved if he will only recite the Buddha's name with faith before his head is finally separated from his trunk: "Recite the Nembutsu, then, and let the sound of this saw against your flesh and bones be like the sound of gongs and wooden drums in a temple liturgy." Western readers in particular may be startled or offended at such a blending of barbarous cruelty, aesthetic refinement, and religious sensibility. But this kind of shocking juxtaposition is a central feature of Umehara's writings, very evident also in his earlier plays for the Kabuki stage, *Yamato-takeru* and *Oguri Hangan*. Umehara generally delights in challenging the conventions and breaking the taboos of contemporary Japanese culture. The Western reader, therefore, must not be too shocked if his or her own taboos are violated, or rather, simply ignored. The grand tradition of liberal humanism, like the lesser canons of "good taste" or "the normal," and contemporary strictures against any arguably value-laden observations based on group differences (whether of gender, ethnicity, or social class) are, none of them, taken as absolute—or, it may be, as very important at all. Thus, Western readers who read attentively should find themselves challenged on several levels by these post-modern medieval Japanese tales.

—The Translator

Heads

When the Steward Nikaidō Masakiyo had been assigned to the province of Bizen some twenty years before, he was told that there had been a "Kingdom of Iron" there in former times. If he recalled that story now, it was because of the discovery of a strange old tumulus.

Since the civil war between the Heike and Genji clans, the world had been in confusion, with robbers impudently going about their business as they liked. They were not content with stealing the possessions of the living; the treasures of the ancient dead who slept in the tumuli were also taken as if by right. And even after the military government was established in Kamakura and a measure of order restored, this particular kind of thievery did not cease.

The land of Bizen has as many ancient tumuli as the provinces of Yamato and Kawachi. The Steward had heard that one of these had been broken into: the interior of the tomb was now visible, and it seemed to be filled with objects made of iron. The Steward wanted to see for himself.

Accompanied by his secretary Enkō, whom he had brought from Kamakura when assigned to the Bizen post, he visited the site. It was true: the tomb had been broken open, and various iron objects were visible through the hole the robbers had made. The Steward ordered his retainers to dig away more earth and excavate the tomb. It turned out to be a huge one, centered on a fine stone chamber with helmets, armor, swords, mirrors, and comma-shaped beads of semiprecious stone. Judging from these funerary objects, it seemed clear that it was the tomb of a king who had once ruled over this region. However, around the dead ruler were ranged, to his right, hoes, scythes, ploughshares and other farming implements, and to his left, weapons of war—swords, halberds, and arrowheads. These were placed close together in an orderly fashion.

Surprised, the Steward asked his secretary, "When was this tomb built? And why are there so many iron objects here?" After pausing to consider, the man answered, "It is a very strange tomb, sir. I've never seen one like it, or read of one either. No doubt the man buried here was the head of the powerful clan who ruled this whole area. He must have held the high rank of *omi* or *muraji* and ruled not only this province of Bizen but the whole land of Kibi. I imagine a king wealthy and powerful enough to contest with the great king of Yamato for hegemony. And it would seem that the basis of his power was iron. I have heard that in ancient times Bizen produced large amounts of iron-sand and that methods of smelting were well developed. Given so much iron and advanced techniques, this ruler would have been able to produce iron implements of excellent quality. He'd have made his country rich by selling things made of iron to other countries. At the same time, his own army would have had the latest sort of good sharp weaponry, and been able to launch campaigns against distant Kanto in the east and Kyushu in the southwest. The land of Kibi may well have surpassed even Yamato itself in power. If the man who sleeps here was indeed a ruler of that sort, I suppose it would have been around the time of the Emperor Nintoku, when Kibi is supposed to have been at its richest and strongest. I can say nothing more about it, ignorant person that I am."

The Steward did not much care for this last "ignorant person that I am" business. No matter what question was put to him, the secretary always ended his reply with this formula, which sounded to the Steward like "I am a learned person—see how much I know! You, I daresay, know very little." But apart from this annoying phrase, the secretary's reply was very satisfactory.

The Steward thought of this hero of former days who had ruled this land through the power of iron. What had he looked like? How many wives did he have? In the midst of such reflections, one idea in particular flitted through his mind: Might it not be possible to create something new by recasting these farm tools and weapons, which looked to be over a thousand years old? As was always the case with him, no sooner had the idea presented itself than he was determined to see it done. He addressed his secretary: "I like these iron things; you can still feel the old ruler's strength of purpose in them. I want to melt them down and make something new. How about it? Do you think it's possible?"

The secretary paused to think before replying: "I have never heard of anyone recasting iron that is over a thousand years old and making something new of it, nor have I read of it being done. Yet I think it is technically possible; and indeed, since it is my lord's command, it must be *made* possible, even if it were not. Fortunately, there are many master swordsmiths in this province of Bizen, and there is one in particular whom I have in mind. He's a bit of an eccentric, but I daresay he'll manage to do the job for us."

The Steward was overjoyed at this news and promptly sent for the master swordsmith. Hearing it was by order of the Lord Steward, he ran so fast he was out of breath, wondering all the while what on earth this august summons might mean. The secretary explained the problem, and the swordsmith, after carefully handling the ancient objects, said to the Steward, "These are wonderful weapons, wonderful farm tools! There must have been a truly great swordsmith in this area, one none of us could equal nowadays. These things are so well made that even after a thousand years, they are still whole. It should be perfectly possible to make new objects from them."

The Steward was a bit stunned to discover that the whim that had entered his mind just a few minutes ago was in fact about to be realized.

"My lord, What is it you wish made from this iron?" asked the swordsmith.

To tell the truth, the Steward wasn't sure. Discomfited by the suddenness of the question, he gave an unexpected reply. "An iron pillar. An iron pillar as big as a man. A gleaming, solid, heavy-weight iron pillar. . . . I leave the exact form to you."

Now both the secretary and the swordsmith were amazed at this demand for an iron pillar; but no more so, perhaps, than the Steward himself, though the demand was his own. However, an order that once issued from the Steward's mouth was not to be countermanded. That would impair the dignity of his office. Noting that the secretary seemed on the verge of saying something, the Steward said, in a once-and-for-all manner, "Right! You're to make me an iron pillar. That's what I want!" What could the secretary and the swordsmith do but say "Yes, my lord," and stand in awe?

The swordsmith began work on the pillar the very next day. First he melted down the old iron. Much of it was in fact corroded, and only a small portion could actually be used. But even so, there was enough remaining from the mass of objects filling the ancient tumulus to make the single iron pillar the Steward desired. The swordsmith carefully considered such matters as what form the pillar should take, and how it ought to be polished. Finally, three months after receiving the order, the swordsmith had the piece done and ready for delivery to the Steward's mansion.

It was truly a strange work of art. So heavy was it, it could not be moved no matter how hard a person might push against it. This iron pillar had a kingly air of authority, with something of the ancient ruler of Bizen about it, and something too of the present Steward (who enjoyed the complete confidence of the Lord Regent in Kamakura). It gleamed with a dull radiance like old silver.

The Steward and his secretary were of course impressed with the results of the swordsmith's labors, but they were bothered somewhat by the pillar's shape. It was long and thick and rounded at the top, closely resembling the male organ.

"Very well done indeed, and worthy of your high reputation as a craftsman. But I'm afraid I don't altogether care for the *shape*. . . ."

The silversmith's response to the Steward's reservation was clever: "Could you be referring to a certain likeness in form to the thing that every man carries on his person? Well, I can't deny there is some resemblance. But, you see, when you're looking for the ideal shape for a pillar, the most beautiful one, this is what you end up with. I didn't intentionally model it on the thing; I just sought out the most perfect form, and it came out looking like this. Now, persons who don't understand about Art might have other ideas of their own, but the truth is that this is the ultimate form achievable in the aesthetic quest!"

Not wishing to lay themselves open to the charge of being "persons who don't understand about Art," the Steward and his secretary had to hold their tongues.

Nevertheless, the Steward was in fact quite proud of this iron pillar of his. When he had guests, he enjoyed explaining to them how it had come to be made. The guests always had a rather strained expression as they said things like, "Well, it certainly is an elegant piece. . . . In its massiveness, its quiet radiance, its. . . . Why, it's just like you yourself, Lord Steward!"

This was the way most visitors responded to the pillar; the Steward's wife, however, had a slightly different reaction. She was five years older than her husband, the daughter of a local official. For a stranger like the Steward to really establish himself in Bizen, it was essential to marry a local girl. And so he had wed her, and she proved to be a very quiet, indeed virtually silent, wife. She being older, he took several young concubines; and she never uttered a word of complaint so long as he showed due respect for her position. The Steward took his wife for granted, like the air he breathed, and devoted himself to his official duties, and to his love affairs.

She was, then, a fine wife for the Steward; but when she saw the iron pillar, a gleam came into her eyes as she said, "I feel some mysterious power in this pillar. . . ." It was in early May that the pillar entered their household. About two months later, on a hot summer's day, the wife suddenly asked if she could borrow it. She sweated easily, and, though summer had hardly begun, the heat was already overwhelming. The Steward himself had begun to wonder uneasily how his perspiration-prone wife would manage to get through this hot season.

"Lend me the pillar for a while. Its cool metal surface will be perfect for fending off this heat. You know how I perspire, so take pity on your poor wife and lend it to me." There was a note of resentment in the way she spoke, resentment at her husband's unbridled passion for his young concubines.

But after all, what difference could it make to the Steward whether the iron pillar stood in his room or his wife's? Far safer, then, to let his wife have the thing than to give her additional cause for complaint. So the iron pillar was duly shifted from his room to hers, and the Steward completely forgot about them both. Occasionally, on an unbearably hot afternoon, he would look in on his wife and find her dozing, propped up against the pillar's cool surface. She was a fastidious woman, and there was nothing unseemly about the way she took her nap. Yet, seeing her there leaning up against the pillar as she slept, the Steward, who had not approached her as his wife for a very long time, felt a sudden erotic urge. "Well, why not, once in a while?" he said to himself as, urged on by lust, he began his approach.

"Just what do you think you're doing? And in broad daylight too! You haven't paid any attention to me for five years, and I don't want it now!" The wife was adamant in her refusal.

In truth, it *had* been five years since the Steward had stopped having relations with his wife. When his passion for his concubines was at its height, she had stubbornly refused all approaches on his part. Having been rebuffed, the Steward decided there was no point in trying to force himself on a woman whose favors were no longer as fresh and intriguing as they had once been. And so physical relations between husband and wife had ended; but apart from that they lived together as before.

It had been a long time, then, since the Steward felt any erotic stirrings toward his wife. But as the hot summer came to an end and the autumn winds began to send a chill through the body, something strange happened. The wife started to show signs of pregnancy. At first the husband thought he must be mistaken, but as the wife's figure grew fuller and fuller, the fact of her pregnancy became clear to everyone. In the midst of the general rejoicing and congratulations, the husband alone knew that he had not touched his wife for a very long time. He went to her room and rebuked her, demanding to know what was going on.

"My, my. Do you imagine I've given myself to another man, perhaps? Well, I haven't; not even once. I'm not sure myself how this happend, but it may be the work of that iron pillar of yours."

"The iron pillar? Do you mean to tell me that that iron pillar could father a child?" The Steward spoke reproachfully, but he knew that she was not the sort of woman who would betray him with another man out of spite. Just to be sure, he questioned her attendants closely about the possible presence of any man, and learned that no other males had been anywhere near his wife's chambers—not only no other man, but not even dogs or tomcats. There are things beyond our understanding, he reflected, and waited for the birth of the child. When the day came, his wife delivered herself of a perfectly round ball of iron.

To the Steward, who had come running at the news that his wife's time had come, she gave the brightest of smiles, saying, "You see, it's just as I said. Now you know that I am a chaste wife who has never given herself to any man but you. This iron ball is the child I saw in my dreams."

The husband picked up this dream child and found it to be a splendid little ball of iron giving off the same dull radiance as the iron pillar made by the master swordsmith. Perhaps it really had been fathered by the pillar, he thought, feeling a slight pang of jealousy at his wife's infidelity, albeit in her dreams.

"You've given birth to a wonderful child! I'm going to make a fine warrior out of it. I'll turn this ball of iron into a sword. After all, the man who made this child's father is a famous swordsmith, so I shall have a splendid sword made from it." This idea, like his earlier one of making an iron pillar, had flashed through his mind as soon as he saw the iron ball. The swordsmith was summoned at once and the Steward, showing him the iron ball, told him to make a sword from it. Naturally, he did not tell the swordsmith how the iron ball had come into his possession, nor was the swordsmith so foolish as to ask. But he must have known at a glance that it had a strong connection with the iron pillar that he had made. At any rate, the swordsmith replied in a perfectly natural manner: "This ball is made of very good iron, so good one would rarely come across it. Given material like this, I must make a really fine sword of it. I look forward to seeing what kind of weapon I can produce. I'm sure it will be the best I've ever made." And with this, he carefully wrapped the iron ball in a carrying-cloth and took it home.

About a year passed. According to the secretary, the swordsmith had remained shut up at home, performing ritual ablutions and working on the sword. When the Steward mentioned this to his wife, she remarked, "My lovely child is going to be a brave warrior. It'll take two or three years, surely." But it didn't. After a little more than a year had passed, the swordsmith appeared at the Steward's residence with the newly crafted sword. Looking forward to seeing what kind of splendid sword had resulted, the Steward began to draw it from its sheath, when the swordsmith stopped him.

"I've been a swordsmith for a long time, but I've never experienced anything as strange as when I made this sword. There were several odd things that happened, but the gods and buddhas must have given their aid to allow me to create this best of all swords. A sword is for slashing people, but this sword does not depend on the swordsman's power to do the slashing. It does it by itself. Bring something close to this sword, and that object will be split in two. Therefore, when you unsheathe it, please be careful to hold it as far from your neck as possible as you examine it."

The Steward thought the swordsmith must be exaggerating; but even so, he kept it far from his neck as he drew it from its sheath. It was truly a wondrous sword! The blade had a mirror-like polish, and the tip was so sharp it seemed almost a living thing. He was about to take a closer look when the swordsmith broke in. "Careful, careful! It's dangerous to bring it close to your body. Your head will be drawn toward the blade and chopped right off!" To prove his point, he brought a sheet of paper close to the blade; it was pulled in and cut in two.

"Heavens!" cried the Steward and the secretary, barely able to speak for amazement.

"There is another strange thing about this sword," the swordsmith continued. "You see how your face is reflected in the blade, my lord? Well, it's your real feelings that are being reflected. Even if you're smiling outwardly, if inside you are angry, then the blade will show an angry face. And if you look very angry but are actually laughing inside, the blade will show a laughing face."

The Steward looked at his face reflected in the blade and saw pure terror.

"You are very frightened right now, my lord, but there is no need for that."

The man is making a fool of me, thought the Steward for a moment; but the more he examined the sword, the more convinced he was of its unique quality. As for the swordsmith's rather rude remark, well, fine craftsmen like him often tended to be eccentrics. Bearing that in mind, he would forgive his rudeness just this once. And how happy he was to have gained this best of all swords from the old iron that emerged from the tumulus.

Early next year, he would be given audience by the Lord Regent in Kamakura. He would show him this sword and repeat what the swordsmith had said just now: how amazed the Regent would be! Having aroused his wonder, the Steward would satisfy it by presenting the sword to His Lordship, and thus ensure his own future prospects. A sly smile spread over the Steward's face. From that day, the precious sword was placed in a box which was to be kept in his own bedchamber.

In the middle of the night on the third day, the Steward suddenly awakened to the sound of someone weeping. It seemed to come from the depths of the earth, this broken-hearted sobbing. It continued for a while, then broke off, then resumed again. At first he thought he was hearing things; but no, it was certainly a human voice. He woke up the young concubine sleeping by his side. "I hear someone crying." The girl opened her eyes sleepily and listened for a while. "It's nothing. You're hearing things," she said, and dropped off again, snoring. The Steward, though, couldn't sleep. Someone was definitely crying—the sound of a man sobbing reached him fragmentarily. He woke the girl up again. "I tell you there is someone crying. Listen." But when the concubine was listening, the voice stopped." You've been dreaming." She went to sleep again, quite unhappy at having been wakened a second time. The Steward lay awake till morning, worrying about that voice.

The next night the same thing happened. This time the Steward listened hard and tried to find the place where the voice was coming from. At first it seemed to be coming from far underground and was very hard to trace. But then he decided it was coming from the box in which the wondrous sword was placed. As he approached the box, the sound of crying became a little clearer, and as he moved away, it became fainter. Could the sword itself be crying?

Next morning he summoned his secretary and discussed the matter. Having heard his master's account, the secretary replied at once: "There are numerous accounts of swords making sounds in the Chinese classics. It is said that a sword made by the noted master Wang Hsin at the command of Emperor Wu of the Han dynasty wept loudly night after night. Then there was the monk Fa Lien of the Eastern Ch'in. A certain sword kept in the king's storehouse would often cry, until Fa Lien pacified its spirit and made it stop. In either case, the sword was crying because it missed another sword. There were originally a pair of swords, you see, male and female. When separated, they cry out of longing for one another, but the male cries more intensely.

"You said that it sounded like a male voice; and I am sure that this is the male of the pair, weeping and yearning for its mate, just as the stag cries for the doe. You recall, I'm sure, the poem about the lonely stag that appears in the collection *A Hundred Poems by a Hundred Poets*—the one by Sarumaru that goes "Walking over crimson leaves in the deep mountains, hearing the voice of the stag crying—how sad is autumn." It expresses the pathos of the sound of the stag crying out for its mate. Could it be that the voice you heard, my lord, was the cry of the sword in its loneliness, like to that of the male deer?"

The Steward felt mild irritation at this somewhat pedantic exposition on the part of his secretary but asked, "Well then, where is this other, female sword?"

"I suspect the swordsmith has it. He must have made two swords, planning to present both of them to your lordship. But then, seeing how splendidly they had turned out, he wanted to keep one of them for himself. Fine craftsmen often feel great attachment to their own works."

The Steward was enraged to hear this and immediately sent retainers off to arrest the swordsmith, but by the time they reached his house, he had already fled and was nowhere to be found. They browbeat his terrified wife and children and ransacked the house, but the female sword they were looking for was gone. No doubt he had learned somehow that the Steward knew he was hiding the other sword and had made off with it. When the retainers returned and made their report to the Steward, he was filled with chagrin. "I'll find that swordsmith if I have to beat the bushes to do it. When I've got him, I'll chop off his head and then take possession of that female sword!"

He scoured not only Bizen but also the neighboring provinces with the help of their stewards; but the swordsmith was nowhere to be found.

Then one day some years later, a traveller brought news of the fugitive. The traveller had gone, he said, to the village of Noshiro in the land of Dewa in the far north and there had encountered someone who seemed to be the swordsmith. He had changed his name, of course, but the excellence of his work was the talk not only of Dewa but of the northern and eastern provinces generally. The secretary, hearing this news, at once reported it to the Steward, who said, "It must be him. And what a cheeky fellow he is, to be boldly carrying on with the same craft, even in far-off Dewa. Go, get hold of the second sword, and bring him back with you. If he refuses, kill him and bring his head back along with the sword."

This was his master's command, and the secretary could not but obey.

As he neared Dewa and began to hear talk of the celebrated craftsman, it became clear that he was known throughout the whole land, though under a different name. The secretary doubted that it could be the same man. If it were he, why would he have carried on his work in such a way that anyone could guess his real identity? It would be as if he were waiting for his whereabouts to become known to the Steward, and for the hands of his pursuers to reach out and take him.

Arriving in Noshiro, he visited the house where the craftsman was living. He announced his name to a servant who came to the door, and then was startled to see the swordsmith appear with a smile on his face. Looking at the secretary, he said, "I understand. The Steward has ordered you to take me back to Bizen, along with the sword. But I can't go back, having done such a shameful thing. It's true: I made a pair of swords, male and female, from the iron ball. Of course I meant to give both of them to the Steward, but they were so fine I just had to keep one back. So I chose the female, little dreaming that the other sword would cry out in the night. They say a fine sword has a spirit of its own, and I'm sure a spirit lodged itself in those splendid swords I made. To have created even one sword in which an august spirit takes up residence is the greatest honor and joy for a swordsmith. So when I heard that the sword wept in the night, I was thrilled. Having made a sword like that, I felt I could die contented. I didn't care if the Steward in his anger had me killed. But I did feel that, since I had the ability, I wanted to make more wonderful swords before I died. That's why I fled. I chose this province because I wanted to do good work in this last, most distant part of Japan. Luckily, there is good-quality iron here, and I was able to make several fine swords that will last for generations to come. I knew that my fame would spread both within and beyond this province, and someday even as far as Bizen; and that the Steward would send men after me. I was afraid of that day, yet at the same time I awaited it. I have been able to do good work in these last few years, so I have no regrets."

The swordsmith brought out from an inner room the other sword that he had made from the iron ball in Bizen and showed it to the secretary. He examined it, taking care to keep it as far from his neck as possible. It was as fine a sword as the one in the Steward's possession.

"Take this sword back with you. Of course, without my head as well, the Steward will never be content. I'll go into the inner room now and chop my head off. You'll hear a noise; when it's quiet again, come into the room."

The swordsmith took the sword with him into the next chamber. After a few moments, there was a sudden sharp cry and the sound of something thudding to the floor. Then it was quiet. Entering the room, the secretary found upon a stand the naked, unsheathed sword, and next to it the swordsmith's head. Beneath the stand were the sheath and the corpse. How had he managed to cut off his own head? At any rate, there would be trouble if the servants came now, so the secretary speedily wrapped the head in a carrying-cloth, holding the sword under his arm, and left the house.

And so he started on his journey back to Bizen; but as he progressed, he noticed something peculiar. The head which he had been carrying with him from Dewa showed not the slightest signs of withering or putrefaction. Now a human body after death gives off a strong smell, and he had worried that the stench of the head on such a long journey would give him away. But far from rotting or smelling, the head looked fresher with every passing day. In addition, though it had had a rather melancholy expression when he looked at it immediately after the swordsmith's death, it now seemed to be regaining its vitality day by day, and to glare at the secretary whenever he took a timid peek at it.

He was amazed and at a loss to understand what was happening. Soon he was too terrified to risk even a peek and simply carried the thing back to Bizen. Going directly to the Steward's mansion, he reported having fulfilled his mission and placed before his master the sword in its box and the head wrapped in cloth. The Steward thanked him for his trouble and rejoiced at now having the matched pair of swords. Opening the box and keeping the sword well away from his neck, as the late swordsmith had urged, he examined the weapon. "This too is a fine sword. And now they're a pair again, husband and wife. Let's give them a formal wedding ceremony tomorrow!" Putting the sword back in its box, he made as if to undo the carrying-cloth: "Since the fellow was able to make something this fine, I suppose he found it hard to give it up. At any rate, he was a great fool. How did he die?"

"It's very strange, actually," the secretary hurriedly began. "On the trip back from Dewa, his head neither putrefied nor withered; it became fresher and livelier, like the head of a living person. I've been too frightened to inspect it for the past few days—it may well be even more lifelike now."

"Neither putrefied nor withered? Don't be stupid! Here, let me have a look at it." He undid the cloth and found the head was indeed fresher and more lifelike than it had been, according to the secretary, five or six days before. Not only that, its eyes were open and glaring balefully at the Steward. He was amazed and cried out in a slightly tremulous voice: "It resents me! But *you* were in the wrong—I showed you favor and then you went and stole the sword. You betrayed me! When the secretary came for you, you'd resigned yourself to die, hadn't you? Well, then, why these angry looks?"

At these words, the head seemed to display a faint smile and continued to stare at the Steward.

"Destroy this head!" cried the Steward to his followers. Yet strange to tell, the head could not be burned with fire nor cut with a sword, almost as if it were made of iron; and its eyes kept staring sadly at the Steward. "Destroy that head!" he screamed, forgetting himself in his rage and terror. Unable to bear the sight of his master in such a state, the secretary broke in: "This must be some sort of curse connected with the ancient iron. We must borrow the power of the spirit of the ancient iron to pacify the vengefulness of the swordsmith's head, now possessed by that spirit. Hard as it may be to do, we must melt down the two swords and the iron pillar he made, and throw the head into the molten iron. It will melt, become smoke, and leave this earth. So it is written in one of the ancient Indian classics."

The Steward did not believe that things like this were in fact written in one of the ancient Indian classics; but at least it was a method worth trying, so he fell in with the secretary's plan and decided to sacrifice the iron pillar and pair of swords. A large kettle was prepared and the three iron objects thrown in. They quickly liquefied in the heat of the blazing fire. When the molten iron was on the boil, they threw in the head.

However, contrary to their expectations, the head did not burn. In the midst of the seething liquid metal it remained unchanged, staring sadly and silently at the Steward, like a living person with a grievance. The gaze he now turned toward his secretary was itself full of accusation.

"What's the meaning of this, Enkō? It's not happening the way you said: the head's not melting and turning to smoke."

The secretary was upset at the Steward's rebuke and said

something surprising even to himself. "I'm sorry, my lord. Apparently here in Japan things don't go just the way they do in the Indian classics. I really do apologize. But there is another method, a good method in cases of this kind, also found in the Indian classics. Cut off my head and toss it into the boiling metal. Then I will be able to talk to the swordsmith's head and clear away all this vengefulness. I am a monk as well as a scholar, after all, and I can certainly do that much. Please command me to do that service for you."

The Steward recalled how the secretary had first come to his family. He had been about seven years old when one day a child was found abandoned in front of the family mansion. The maids had taken him to look, and it had turned out to be a boy-child dressed in rags. After a while his father came along and ordered that the boy be taken in and raised. Even now he could hear the crying of the abandoned boy and the voice of his father ordering him to be taken in. His father had recognized the boy's cleverness and, thinking he would at some point be of help to his own son, had sent him to study at the "Five Mountains," centers of Buddhist and Chinese learning. There he acquired a reputation as a scholar-monk; but when the son was appointed Steward of Bizen, the father ordered the foundling-turned-priest to accompany him as his secretary.

Even in Bizen, though, the secretary was always reading books. Of course he did not marry, and he never gave rise to the least whisper of scandal. The Steward was not sure what his secretary thought or felt in his heart, nor did he particularly care. But this unexpected offer now made him think again about the other's life. Perhaps he felt under obligation at having been raised and educated, and had decided to sacrifice himself in repayment.

The Steward did not want to accept this extraordinary

request, but the secretary was determined and showed no signs of allowing himself to be diverted. Then too, there was the intractable problem of the swordsmith's head still staring at the Steward from the midst of the molten iron as it seethed and bubbled. It was really too bad, but perhaps he ought to go along with the idea after all....

"Well then, shall we have your head tossed into the pot, as you suggest?"

The secretary was overjoyed: "Now, I'll stretch my neck out over the pot like so, and you chop off my head and drop it in." The Steward steeled himself against pity and cut off the secretary's head, which fell with a plop into the molten iron.

The two heads were now facing one another in the pot. For a time they just floated there, staring at each other.

How long did this situation last? Not very long—perhaps five or ten minutes. But to the Steward who was watching with bated breath to see what would happen, it seemed of infinite duration. The two heads continued to stare at one another, and then there was the sound of loud laughter, like the rumbling of heaven and earth. The two heads were laughing.

"Strange!" The Steward turned toward the secretary's head to administer a rebuke. "This is not at all what you suggested. You were to get into the pot of boiling metal and convince the swordsmith's head to rest in peace. What is the meaning of this raucous laughter from the pair of you?"

The two heads looked at the Steward with mocking smiles.

"What! You're making sport of me? You never dared look at me like that when you were alive. I'll have you cut into little pieces!" The Steward was so excited he leaned right out over the kettle. At that point something very strange happened. His head detached itself from his body and dropped into the kettle. It floated on the surface of the molten iron and glared angrily at the other two heads. The swordsmith's head, as before, stared back at the Steward's with a melancholy gaze, while the secretary's looked at him in a clearly mocking manner.

For a while the three-cornered staring continued. Then the Steward's head bit into the swordsmith's and the swordsmith's head into his. The secretary's head entered in, trying to break the fight up, only to be bitten by both of the other two. It then launched a fierce counterattack against both of them. For the next two or three hours the interior of the kettle was transformed into a veritable hell of fighting demons. Eventually, though, the three heads became exhausted, and quiet returned to the kettle. The heads were so torn and bloodied that one could hardly tell which was which, yet each of them wore a faint smile of triumph. Then, still smiling, the three heads began to dissolve in the seething molten iron until they disappeared without a trace.

Haseo's Love

One day, as Ki no Haseo was returning alone from court, he noticed someone following him. Observant as always, Haseo had known for some time that he was being followed. Whether aware of that or not, the other continued to follow; and Haseo decided to wait for the fellow at a certain corner. He turned out to be a small, strangely thin man sporting a little mustache—an ordinary-looking sort, on the whole.

"You've been following me for some time now. Why?"

"Well, well, so I've been found out. You can't put anything over on Ki no Haseo, can you? I have some business to discuss with you," replied the man in a composed manner.

"Business with me? What business?"

"I have a small favor to ask of Lower Third Rank Middle Councilor Ki no Haseo, known to everyone in the capital as a man powerful enough to bring down a bird on the wing with a mere glance."

Haseo was bothered by this last expression. True, he was a Middle Councilor of the Lower Third Rank; but that did not imply the power to "bring down a bird on the wing." On the contrary, Haseo doubted he could manage to bring down even a perching bird. But the man continued, "You are, after all, the foremost disciple of the late Sugawara no Michizane. What a pitiful way to have died! But now he's a god who can send down terrible curses upon men, isn't he? And you alone, they say, can actually communicate with this fearsome deity, Master Haseo!"

To be sure, Haseo was a disciple of Michizane. Like him, he was a brilliant graduate of the University. He had learned a good deal from Michizane, whose specialty was of course literature. But Haseo had pursued many other studies as well: the Chinese Way of Yin and Yang, the *Book of Changes*, mathematics, and other somewhat dubious fields. But his master Michizane had, some ten years before, been exiled to Dazaifu in northern Kyushu, shortly after achieving the high position of Minister of the Right, Lower Second Rank. This had been, of course, the work of his enemy Fujiwara no Tokihira, Minister of the Left, who feared an increase in Michizane's power. Michizane was partial to talented officials who, like himself, had risen through passing the government examinations. Such "scholars-turned-officials" were the recipients of his favor. Tokihira was not pleased with this, for what would become of the privileges of the well born? To him, intent on supporting the dictatorship of the northern branch of the Fujiwara clan under the guise of the regency system, Michizane's existence seemed a threat. That was why he fabricated a case against him and had him banished to Dazaifu. At the time, everyone supposed that Ki no Haseo would also be sent into exile as Michizane's chief disciple. Tokihira, however, punished only Michizane and his children in an effort to limit the effects of the incident as much as possible. And, contrary to the general expectation, Haseo rose in rank rather than losing his position. This was a clever political move on Tokihira's part: He knew that Haseo was not the type ever to oppose anyone in authority and so decided to make him his ally; by doing so, he would also gain a reputation as a wise and generous statesman. Of course, it placed Haseo in a delicate position as Michizane's favorite student. He had a good grasp of his situation, though, and managed outwardly to display appropriate sympathy for his master while inwardly giving his loyalty to Tokihira.

Then, after Michizane died an angry exile in Dazaifu, it was widely rumored that his vengeful ghost was cursing Tokihira and those around him. People trembled at the awful power of Michizane's spirit, particularly after a thunderbolt struck the palace, killing many of the courtiers who had been involved in the banishment. Tokihira himself declared his sturdy indifference to anything the spirit of a mere Minister of the Right might do against him, Minister of the Left; but the other members of his family were seized with the most abject terror. Through it all, Ki no Haseo's position at court grew stronger and stronger, for he was the only one who, it was thought, could console Michizane's outraged ghost and bring an end to the curse. Thus it was that he was made Middle Councilor of the Lower Third Rank.

He had attained a position higher than he had ever hoped for, but he was also lonely and bored. A man who communes closely with a god, especially an angry one, is generally avoided.

The man broke in on these thoughts of Haseo's with the remark, "Master Haseo, I have heard you are an expert in many fields, including gambling. They say there's nothing you don't know about the subject of gambling, ancient and modern, from east to west. And not only in theory but in practice as well, you are the greatest gambler of the age—is it not so?"

Haseo was amazed to hear the terms "theory" and "practice" from the mouth of this fellow, for it was precisely in the unity of theory and practice that both his scholarship and that of his master Michizane had discovered their ideal goal. Michizane is often considered a master primarily of literature, but this is a mistake. If it were only a matter of literature, there were, and probably are, greater figures than he. His true greatness lay in his ability to use all branches of learning, including literature, for political ends. Without that, how could someone from the scholarly Sugawara clan have succeeded in becoming Minister of the Right, one of the most powerful men in the land? He not only used his learning for political purposes, but was able at the same time to maintain a useful distinction between the scholar and the politician. When there was a political confrontation he wished to avoid, he would say he was, after all, a scholar, and stand aside. Not, of course, that he stood *completely* aside. Rather, he gave the appearance of standing apart as a scholar while reading the signs of the times so as to be able to end up on the winning side. This was the secret of his success and the way he became Minister of the Right. But this success was ultimately his downfall. Even the ever-prudent Michizane could not resist the temptation of a rank higher than he could ever have dreamt of. At any rate, it was by linking theory and practice that Michizane had been able to succeed; and Haseo, as his student, had thoroughly mastered this lesson in getting on in the world. If, unlike Michizane, he had devoted himself to the study of Yin-Yang, the *Book of Changes*, mathematics, and gambling, it was because he wished to learn things of practical benefit.

"Yes, well, I have made a little study of gambling, as you suggest."

"Hardly 'a little study,' sir. They say you're the most skillful gambler at court, do they not?"

It was as the man said: Haseo was the best hand at gambling in the palace. He had made a thorough study of the subject, reading every book he could lay his hands on, whether old or new, from east or west. He had paid careful attention to backgammon, just then very popular among the nobility. (This was different from contemporary backgammon, with a far greater element of risk.) From a very young age, he became a skilled player, with Fujiwara no Nagatoshi, Captain of the Guards of the Right, Kiyowara no Sadasuke, head of the Household Secretariat, and Tachibana no Shigeie, of the Secretariat of State, as companions. As leader of the group, Haseo would invite his friends over to his house to play backgammon till dawn. It would have looked bad to have all-night gambling sessions at the house of a scholar, however, so they told their families they had organized a study-circle. After all, no one would expect them to be playing backgammon at the house of Ki no Haseo, the most distinguished scholar then at court. Some of the wives may have suspected an assignation with a secret mistress, but they diplomatically chose to say nothing. And so the all-night sessions went unnoticed by the other courtiers.

Except for Michizane. "They say you've organized a study-circle lately. What're you studying, if I may ask? Word has it that it's something to do with numbers. . . . What could it be? At any rate, you'd do well to be careful of gossip."

Startled at Michizane's insightfulness, Haseo answered lamely, "Oh no, I'm not the sort who'd do anything on the sly." Michizane smiled faintly as if to say, "I know exactly what you and your friends are up to." He was warning Haseo to be careful of gossip, but the disciple for his part was worried about certain rumors regarding the master. Michizane was a skilled painter as well as littérateur, and there was said to be a very unseemly painting by him of a certain woman, almost totally nude. The woman in the painting looked exactly like one of the Retired Emperor Uda's consorts, even to the appearance of a mole on a portion of the inner thigh. Now Michizane was almost as great a womanizer as he was a writer. He had many wives and concubines, and children from them; and in addition there were rumors linking him with numerous other women. The new rumor about the woman in the painting was perhaps credible given Michizane's nature, but it seemed to Haseo likely to have been made up and put about by his master's enemies, and to be highly dangerous. He had been meaning to tell Michizane about the rumor and warn him to exercise care, but it was hard to broach the subject. So he had remained silent until now, when *he* was being warned to guard *his* reputation. How odd it felt!

"You're the one who should be careful!" The words had risen to his lips but he was able to choke them back. Shortly afterwards, Michizane was banished. "I probably should have said something at the time," reflected Haseo, as the entire series of events flashed through his consciousness in a kind of panorama.

"Middle Councilor, I would very much appreciate the favor of a game with you." The words brought Haseo back to the here and now. "I've just got hold of a splendid backgammon set that belonged to the late Lord Keeper of the Privy Seal. I'd like to play one game with you using that set. Of course, I know I can't win, but won't you help me inaugurate my new set with a game? It would be a supreme honor for me."

Haseo was intrigued by this sudden, unexpected proposition, in part because he was bored. Day after day, he found himself with time on his hands, so it might be entertaining to have a game with this fellow using the Lord Privy Seal's personal set.

"All right, I'll accept your invitation for a game. Now, what day shall we make it?"

"Why, today, of course. 'Hasten to do a good thing,' as the proverb says! We could start right now."

"Right now? That's a little too soon. What about tomorrow?"

"By tomorrow, you may not feel like doing it."

Haseo was beginning to feel his old passion for gambling rising within, for the first time in a long while. The long-dead excitement of his youthful days came back to life, and he could not bring himself to refuse. "Well, since I'm free until evening today, I'll accept."

"Thank you, sir! You've fulfilled my greatest wish. The backgammon set itself should rejoice," said the man, already starting to walk. "My house is just nearby. Please follow me."

Haseo followed along after the man, who kept a swift pace as he moved steadily southward. They passed Third Avenue, then Fourth, then Fifth and Sixth, until at last they came to Ninth Avenue.

"Your house is a good distance, not 'just nearby' as you said. Why, this is Ninth Avenue, at the southern edge of the capital, near the Rashōmon gate!"

The cities of Japan are not surrounded by fortified walls, like those in China, so their gates have lost their original significance as points of entry and exit for the inhabitants. Since one can enter the city from anywhere, the gate functions not as a proper entrance way but as a mere sign that from here the city begins. So it was that soon after the construction of the capital the Rashōmon fell into dilapidation and in time became known as the haunt of robbers.

"This is where I live," said the man as he climbed up the staircase leading to the upper story of the gate.

Could he be a robber? Apart from his extraordinary thinness, there was nothing to differentiate him from anyone else. No, he just didn't seem the robber type. And what if he was? Reminding himself that he did want to play backgammon right now, Haseo followed the man up the stairs.

The interior of the second story looked liked the sitting room in a nobleman's mansion. It was carefully furnished and incense was burning.

"Not a bad place, is it? And there's a fine view of the capital from here," said the man, indicating the direction Haseo should look. And indeed it was a superb view.

"A wonderful view! This place is far better than my mansion."

"No, no, you mustn't flatter me like that. I like it, though; it suits me, dubious sort of fellow that I am. Well now, shall we have a little game? But it's no fun to play without betting something; and betting money seems a little dull, doesn't it? So I was thinking, how would this be: You're almost certain to win, but if by some chance I do, I'd ask you to destroy the records on file with the police concerning one 'Demon' Tarō. I know you're on very close terms with the commissioner, Taira no Yasuhira. This 'Demon' Tarō fellow is not in police hands at this point, and I have some little connection with him. And anyway, he never committed the crime he's accused of in those records. But it'd be hard to prove his innocence, and that's why I'd like those records destroyed. Now Taira no Yasuhira served under you at one point, sir, and I've heard that he'd do anything you asked. There's not a chance in a thousand you'd lose to me; but, just in case, could I have your help with this matter?

"Now, what about if you win? You don't need money from the likes of me, so I thought I'd present you with something quite rare—the most beautiful woman in the world. Her skin is incredibly white, almost transparent in fact. Her hair is long and black, her eyes large and dark, her lips red as could be; and set between those eyes and those lips is a charming little nose. I'm sure you've never seen a woman as beautiful as this. And if I lose, I'll deliver her to you myself."

Haseo didn't believe everything the man told him; but if he did lose, it would be a simple matter to destroy this 'Demon' Tarō fellow's records. Taira no Yashuhira was a cooperative man, after all. So he didn't see how he could lose much by this bet. And if he won, the most beautiful woman in the world might be his!

"If I win, you're going to give me this most beautiful of women, correct?"

"Yes, I swear it before you, Master Haseo, and the gods of Kumano. So, let us begin."

The two sat down in front of a backgammon board and began to play. At first, both had wins and losses but gradually Haseo began to lose steadily. Most men lose their nerve in a situation like this, but not Haseo. A skilled politician never acts irrationally no matter how bad things get. The same principle holds with gambling, so no matter how badly things were going for him, Haseo never lost control. Knowing that in essence gambling and politics were the same, he applied himself to a calm consideration of why it was he kept on losing. Was the other man cheating? He called to mind all the different ways of cheating at backgammon that he knew of, from every age and land, but none of them seemed to fit. So he continued to lose, till evening came, and then night.

"My loss. Today I've done nothing but lose. I'm no match for you, my friend, and it's time I was going home. I'll have 'Demon' Tarō's records expunged from the police files, as agreed."

But as Haseo rose to leave, the other man said, "You've just been unlucky so far. The game has just begun! Let's play till dawn. I hear you've often done so in the past."

Haseo in fact did not like leaving after such a string of losses, but he knew his family would be worried if he didn't get home soon. As he tried to leave, the man, sensing his reluctance, quickly suggested, "Of course we'll have to let your family know you'll be out all night. I can send a messenger."

"I can't say I'm going to be spending the night playing backgammon!"

"What about using a directional taboo as an excuse? Say you're spending the night with a friend to avoid traveling home in an unlucky direction."

The belief in lucky and unlucky directions was a part of the Way of Yin and Yang, often made good use of by the aristocrats of this age when they wished to spend the night with another woman. Haseo agreed to the proposal and sent off a messenger, having decided to play backgammon till dawn if necessary.

"Well, let's get to it. Or would you perhaps like something to fortify yourself with first? Some good food and saké should restore your energies." As if from nowhere, servants appeared bearing great platters filled with delicacies from land and sea. It all looked wonderfully delicious, but Haseo had no mind for food at that moment: All he could think of was backgammon, and why on earth he had lost so much. If not the other's cheating, then what was it? Aha! thought Haseo. Whenever he shakes the dice, he makes an odd sound, like "Eh!" It must have some magical power. . . . I have to do something before he manages to say "Eh!"

Having finished eating, the two once again began their game. At first, each man sometimes won and sometimes lost, just as before; but then the tide turned strongly against

Haseo. Sure enough, the man kept on making that sound. Haseo decided to act. Before the man could say "Eh!" as he shook the dice, Haseo cried "Ya!" Was it because of that that the man's hand began to tremble as he shook the dice? At any rate, Haseo won that throw. From then on, Haseo made sure to slip in a "Ya!" before the other could say "Eh!" The man began to lose steadily, until his losses far outweighed Haseo's before dinner. Of course, the other man kept on crying his belated "Eh!"s as he shook the dice, but it was no use: he never beat Haseo again.

Finally it was morning. "Well, the new day's here," said Haseo.

"I've lost, I'm sorry to say. It's the first time this has ever happened to me. A total loss for me." The man looked very regretful. "Now I won't be able to save 'Demon' Tarō." He seemed on the verge of tears. Haseo wondered if perhaps this 'Demon' Tarō was, not a relative or close friend of the man, but the man himself. He began to feel sorry for him, and tried to cheer him up: "Don't worry. I promise I'll look into the 'Demon' Tarō matter sometime soon."

That seemed to make the other feel much better: "I'd appreciate that very much. And I'll be sure to deliver the woman to you, sir. At twilight five days from now, I'll bring you the most beautiful woman in the world. Where would you like her brought?"

"To my villa—I mean, my study-house." This "study-house" was in fact Haseo's villa; and, though of course he used it as a place for quiet study, in his younger days he had also entertained women there, unbeknownst to his wife. He had an old serving-woman staying there, one who knew how to keep a secret.

"The study-house is close by Kiyomizu Temple. Please bring her there."

"Of course, sir."

Haseo said good-bye and returned home.

Five days had passed. It was not as if Haseo had been waiting and longing for the promised day to come. He didn't put much faith in what the man had said, but if it turned out to be true, all the better. He had enjoyed his game of backgammon (the first in a long time), and he had seen the marvelous view of the capital from the top of the Rashōmon. So it really didn't much matter whether the fellow's story was true or false. But as twilight drew on, he began to think about the promise, and decided at any rate to go to his villa and wait. As he did so, his heart beat faster, as it had when he had his first experience with a woman, a good many years before. Even with age, it didn't change, this excitement at a first encounter.

After perhaps two hours had passed, the man appeared, as promised, with the woman. Looking at her, Haseo was amazed, for it was just as the man had said. Her skin was, indeed, not simply exceedingly white, but almost translucent. Her black hair fell in long waves nearly to her ankles, and her eyes shone with a mysterious depth. Her lips were a deep crimson color, and above them was a small, charming nose. Haseo had never seen anyone so beautiful. He led the two visitors into the sitting-room, and in the dim light looked again, carefully, at the woman. She was indeed very beautiful, yet there was about her something not of this world. She seemed to radiate a mysterious light, which made Haseo recall the stories he had read about Hsi Shih, the fabled beauty of ancient China.

"I have brought the woman as promised, Master Haseo. She is, as I said, the most beautiful of women, is she not? You may do with her as you like, but there is one condition I must ask you to observe. For the next one hundred days, you must not sleep with her. If you violate this condition, she will simply vanish. Now, I know it seems cruel to bring you a beautiful girl like this and then ask you to wait a hundred days. But on the other hand, you are well known for your fortitude and self-control, so I am sure you will keep the condition and wait patiently. After a hundred days have passed, you are free to do absolutely anything you like. So please bear up; pile endurance upon endurance, and wait out the hundred days. It's agreed, then. On no account forget what I have told you."

The man left after uttering these seemingly highly significant words, and Haseo was left alone with the woman. She had been listening silently to what was said, but seemed unaffected both by the man's words and by his departure. Nor did she show the least sign of fear at being left alone with Haseo. From that night she became a resident of the villa. She spent her days locked away in her room and seemed very much averse to going out into the sunlight. Haseo was curious about her past and tried questioning her about it, but she would not answer. He supposed she had gone through some very trying times, but he had no way of learning anything specific. The woman was by no means stupid: she understood everything that was said to her and carried out Haseo's commands to the letter. Yet he had no idea what she might be thinking, or rather, feeling, for she seemed to have no emotions at all. Actually, this rather excited Haseo. There was something hidden deep inside her, and he wanted to touch that something. He enjoined absolute secrecy on the old serving-woman so no one could know of the woman's existence, not his wife, not his children, no one. He made a point of visiting his villa once every three days, and of spending the night there once a week. Those nights were hard on him. Thinking of her lying there under the same roof, he found it impossible to sleep. It would be a simple matter to make her his own. She was perfectly compliant, never opposing him in anything.

If he tried to sleep with her, no doubt she would accept his advances in silence. Having wrestled with himself for some time, he decided one night to steal into her room. Yet when he arrived in front of her sliding door, his legs would carry him no further.

"Wait one hundred days. If you take her before the hundred days are up, she will vanish." The man's warning still rang in his ears. They were like a heavy weight about his legs as he prepared to sneak into the woman's bedchamber. How many times had Haseo gone as far as her door, recalled those words, and then returned to his own room with a heavy heart? Sometimes he did this several times in a single night.

Night after night was spent like this; and as twenty days passed, then one month, Haseo began to show signs of fatigue. It was hard for him to face the woman in the morning after one of these sleepless nights. The woman, for her part, would greet him as if nothing at all were the matter and serve his breakfast. Could she have known how often he came to her room at night, hesitated, and withdrew? It would seem she must have, but she gave no sign of it whatsoever. Haseo felt he understood her less and less, yet was drawn to her more and more uncontrollably.

By the time the sixtieth day had passed, he had grown very haggard. There began to be rumors about him at court: "Haseo goes to his villa and holds communication with the dead Michizane—I'm sure of it! That's why he looks so ill and exhausted."

The people in power began to be afraid of him and to avoid his company. Thus, Haseo grew still more lonely, and the lonelier he was, the more obsessed he became with the woman. The seventieth day came and went, and he felt he could not hold up any longer. Then, on precisely the eightieth day after the woman's arrival, Haseo said to himself, "The fellow said one hundred days; but a full eighty days have passed. . . . Surely there could be no harm in sleeping with her now!" In the realm of practical affairs, Ki no Haseo was the most rational of men. If the man had warned him to wait one hundred days, there was probably a good reason for doing so. The Haseo of former days would have understood that and waited. But now everything was different: he'd gone mad with love. One hundred days was too long; eighty was his limit. Hadn't eighty percent of the specified time passed? It would be all right. Besides, the man had, no doubt, deliberately inflated the number. Thus, Haseo interpreted things as he wished and decided to sleep with the woman. His vaunted reasoning powers were unable to prevent it.

That night he had dinner with the woman, got very drunk on saké, and urged some on her as well. As she drank, her skin became whiter and whiter, more and more translucent; her hair, blacker; and her lips, a deeper red. Haseo could control himself no longer; drawing her close, he led her to where he slept. She went willingly enough, with no show of resistance. Haseo went briefly to the bathroom and then came back to find to his surprise that she had already undressed and was waiting for him under the quilts. Pulling back the top-quilt, he saw she was stark naked. And what a wondrous nakedness it was! Her skin, more translucent than simply white, allowed each vein to show faintly through; it almost seemed as if one might catch a dim glimpse even of her inner organs. No, she could not be a creature of this world. She seemed more like a wax doll lying there. It was beyond mere beauty; it was mystery. Her nakedness did not fail to arouse Haseo's desire. Her deep red lips were most inviting; her breasts were rich and full, and of course translucent.

He embraced her, and she submitted meekly to everything he wished to do. When at last their two bodies had become one, she gave a faint cry. Haseo was in his fifties and knew all there was to know about the love of women, but never had he experienced such pleasure as he did now. It was a strange sensation: he felt himself become a massive phallus wrapped round by crimson clouds and slowly dissolving within them. In the midst of this intensely pleasurable sensation, sleep fell upon him. It was only for a few seconds, an instant or two in which he did not so much sleep as simply close his eyes. But in that instant, the woman he had been holding in his arms had vanished. Astonished, he looked about the room, but the woman was not to be found. He felt a kind of chill, and then saw that the place where she had lain was covered with water. And the water was moving. Following its flow, he watched it move as if in flight toward the passageway. The woman had turned to water, flowed out into the passage, and disappeared.

Shaken, Haseo hurried to wake up the serving-woman: "She's gone! Do you know anything about it?" How could the old woman have known? But still he kept asking her.

"She must've run off somewhere, sir. You never paid much attention to her, after all."

"No, no, she was just here. Look, here are her robes!"

"You must be joking, sir. These are the very robes she was wearing when she come here. Do you mean to say the robes are still here but the girl inside them has up and vanished? Come now, sir."

For some time thereafter Haseo was a mere shell from which the living spirit seemed to have departed. He continued to go to court everyday, maintaining the habits of a diligent official; but even there his strange behavior attracted attention. The courtiers whispered among themselves that Haseo's intercourse with Michizane had gone too far, that the dead man's soul had taken possession of him.

The empty, spiritless days continued, but Haseo had

begun to recover a little of his composure when one day, on his way back from the palace, he once again encountered the other man. He grabbed hold of him and took him back to his villa. Then, seating him on the very spot where the woman had disappeared, he recounted what had happened. The man listened to what he had to say with a mocking smile, and answered as follows:

"It looks as if you weren't able to bear up after all, Master Haseo. Yes, even you, the most self-controlled man at court, couldn't quite carry it through. Of course, an ordinary man wouldn't last a day with a beautiful woman like that. But you stood it for eighty days. I was proud of you, truly: the greatest disciple of Master Michizane, the man who can commune with gods and spirits, Master Haseo himself! And yet, those last twenty days proved too much for you. You'd waited for eighty long days, but you couldn't wait another twenty? Whereas if you *had* waited only those twenty more days, you could have enjoyed the favors of that gorgeous woman forever!

"Why did she disappear, you ask? Because, you see, she wasn't a human being. It's no wonder she disappeared when you consider how she came to be: I collected corpses from here and there, selected only their best features, and concocted her myself! I'm not a bad craftsman, though I say it who shouldn't, and that woman was my finest creation. After I was finished, I added a soul. In a hundred days time the soul would have attached itself firmly to the body, and my masterpiece would have been complete. In other words, this uniquely beautiful woman, the loveliest creature in the world, would have become a genuine human being. Oh, if you'd only waited another twenty days, just another twenty days! I regret it almost as much as you do. So I guess our little game ended in a draw, hmm? Ha, ha, ha, ha!"

The man laughed loudly, and Haseo thought he'd laugh along to keep him company. Oddly, though, no sound came forth.

"What a loss! If only you'd told me what she was right from the start, I would have been able to bear up for the last twenty days. . . . Well, I suppose it wasn't a total loss, though. I enjoyed a good night's gambling, and one night of pure pleasure with the most beautiful woman in the world, didn't I." Haseo gave a laugh, but the laugh sounded close to a cry. Suddenly coming to himself, he said to the man, as if he'd just remembered to ask, "And who, by the way, are you?"

"Me? A devil is what I am. Remember about 'Demon' Tarō? Well, he's a member of our family. But I was a human being myself, once. I had some things on my conscience, some regrets and the like, when I died, and I ended up a devil. That's how I was able to learn the art of making a beautiful woman from a pile of corpses."

Haseo was not too surprised when he heard this explanation. "You're not at all devilish, you know. You seem very human."

"Seeming very human is absolutely the best thing for a devil. . . . The room at the top of the Rashōmon was an illusion, you know. You climbed a phantom gate, and played backgammon in a phantom room."

The man departed, thanking Haseo politely for his kindnesses. Gazing after him, Haseo felt reminded of someone. He couldn't recall who it was, though, so he decided to go to the Rashōmon, thinking it might help somehow. The gate was there all right, but it was quite different from the Rashōmon where he had played backgammon. It was covered with cobwebs, and the staircase he thought he'd climbed was too rickety by far to bear his weight. Was the Rashōmon where he'd gambled with the man a complete illusion, then? Later on, he had Taira no Yasuhira check the police records for him, just to be sure; but there was no record of a "Demon" Tarō. If, then, "Demon" Tarō did not exist in this world, could the man have been, as he claimed, in truth a devil?

The Nun Oyō

To the west of the capital, near Sagano, there lived a monk, a solitary recluse. He was not yet even forty, but seemed already to have abandoned all hopes of this world. He could not have been of very good family to begin with, but his present state was truly wretched. No one knew how he had lived in his younger days. No doubt he had moved from one kind of work to another, failing at each, until finally ending as a beggar-monk. Now he had settled down in desolate Sagano, west of the capital, and spent his days reciting the *nembutsu*, the holy name of Amida Buddha, praying earnestly for rebirth in the Pure Land of Perfect Bliss.

But there was a story behind his settling there and entering upon the religious life. At a time when everything he touched turned to dust and he had become disgusted with the world, he happened to visit the Seiryō-ji temple in Saga. It was not that he was particularly devout then. The gods and buddhas seemed to him nothing more than shams devised by men unable to face the sorrows of this world. If his

feet turned toward Seiryō-ji, it was only because he was carried along by the flood of pilgrims on their way there. Even so, having come to the temple, he felt he ought to say a prayer, so he dropped the pittance he had into the offering box, made his reverence to the Buddha as custom demanded, and then started on his way again.

"Excuse me! You there, young man. I have something I want to say to you."

It was a male voice, and when he turned around he saw a man in his early fifties standing there, looking as down-at-heels as he himself. For a moment he wondered if his own shadow might have taken on bodily form, so closely did the man resemble him.

"We do look alike, don't we," the man continued. "You're the image of me when I was younger. Poor and wretched-looking—just the way I was! When I saw you worshipping at Seiryō-ji, I was so surprised that I followed you here. You really do look the same." The man laughed as he spoke.

He took another look at the man. He had to admit that, indeed, in their poverty and shabbiness, they were very much alike. No doubt the man had borne more than his share of troubles in this sad world, just as he had. Now, having lost faith in everything within the fleeting world, the man was just passing his days in idleness. In that respect, the two of them were indistinguishable; and yet, the man had something in him that he himself lacked.

"I've been watching you for quite some time. Your soul, it's floating about, you know—not quite attached to your body. It seems to be wandering about somewhere in empty space. Ten years ago, my soul was floating around too, and I always felt unsettled and anxious, just like you. I was very unhappy. And you, you're very unhappy too. But now I'm filled with joy, and I want to give that joy to you, my look-alike!"

"Joy"—the word had not existed for him for close to twenty years now. How could this miserable-looking man give him joy? He had no faith in what the man said.

"It was a monk called Gokuraku Shōnin, from Kasagi, who gave me this joy." The man seemed to gaze into his very soul as he continued: "The saint taught me the joy of reciting the *nembutsu*. If you earnestly invoke the Holy Name, you can be reborn in the Pure Land of Perfect Bliss. And so I put aside all worldly attachments, and now I'm filled with joy at my salvation." The man laughed happily.

Recite the *nembutsu* and be reborn in Paradise—this was the teaching of Saint Hōnen. He knew that, of course; and there were among his acquaintances a good number of *nembutsu* devotees. But when he saw the black-robed monks reciting the Holy Name, he was unpleasantly reminded of a group of crows noisily cawing. He couldn't believe that anyone would gain rebirth by reciting like that. When he realized that this fellow was one of those *nembutsu* zealots, he lost all interest.

But the man continued speaking, his gaze again seeming to penetrate his hearer's soul: "I suppose you think that by '*nembutsu*' I mean the oral *nembutsu*, where you say out loud the words 'Namu Amida Butsu.' But that's an 'accommodated teaching,' designed by St. Hōnen for the guidance of the mass of ignorant people. The *nembutsu* which the saint himself practiced privately is another thing entirely. It's the meditative *nembutsu*, explained in the saint's favorite scripture, the *Sutra of Meditation on the Buddha of Infinite Life*. It teaches that if you meditate upon Lord Amida and his Pure Land of Perfect Bliss, they will be present within you, sleeping and waking; and at the moment of death, you will see Lord Amida coming to welcome you to his Paradise. So your rebirth in the Pure Land is perfectly assured.

"Now the method of meditation is extremely difficult.

What you need above all is concentration of mind. This has nothing to do with intellectual ability. If even a foolish, ignorant man like me was able to acquire it, there is no reason you cannot. There are thirteen stages in the meditation. You begin by visualizing the various aspects of the Pure Land, then the Buddha Amida, Lord of the Pure Land, and finally yourself being born on one of the lotus flowers that bloom in the pond before the Lord Amida.

"I will give you a more detailed explanation of all thirteen stages later, but for now let's begin with the sun meditation. The course of meditation starts with visualizing the setting sun. As you visualize it day after day, your mind and heart will tend naturally toward the direction where the sun sets, that is, toward the West, where the Pure Land lies. When the sun-meditation is finished, you visualize the waters of the Pure Land. When you can clearly see the waters, you visualize the earth. When that is done, you visualize the various trees that grow from the earth of the Pure Land. After the trees become clearly visible, you concentrate on the lotus pond; and after that, the high pavilions, and after that, the throne of Lord Amida. After all these scenes of the Pure Land have become clearly visible, you visualize the figure of the Lord himself. Amida Buddha will appear radiating light, and that dazzling light will illuminate the whole of the Pure Land that you have visualized.

"Next there is another meditation on Amida Buddha. The one I just described is of his appearance to the devotee. Now one visualizes the 'True Body' of Amida, hidden within or beyond the appearance. These last two meditations, the eighth and ninth, are the most essential ones; but then one goes on to visualize Amida's two attendant bodhisattvas, Kannon and Seishi, and then all the multitudes of buddhas and bodhisattvas that exist. Finally, in what is called the meditation on the Body of Perfect Freedom, one visualizes the Buddha manifesting himself freely in a multitude of different forms. And this brings the course of meditation to an end."

The man said all this without pausing once. As the other listened, the Pure Land seemed to appear before him, and Lord Amida was there, and he felt as if he were an infant, just now born upon the lotus petals.

"I continued this holy practice for three years; and in the end, the Pure Land became visible to me in every detail. If I thought of the skies of Paradise, or the earth, or the waters, they appeared before me. I became able to call up the Pure Land in its entirety, just as I wished. I am sure I will be reborn there, and so my life now is full of joy and happiness. I would like to share that happiness with you."

The man was no longer looking at him. He was gazing into the far distance, and on his face was a look of ecstasy. The man looked so happy that the other began to feel the same way and, though he could not believe it was really true, he was willing to join the man in his rosy dream world. And so he decided to take this shabby stranger as his religious master and learn from him how to see the Pure Land of Perfect Bliss while still living in this world.

From then on, the man came everyday to the hovel where the other lived. But the practice turned out to be extremely severe and difficult. The men may have seemed alike, in their poverty and despair of worldly success; but the other quickly realized the gap between the two of them as soon as he began to practice meditation.

Day after day, he devoted himself to imagining the Pure Land; and in time the beautiful land of Paradise began to float into his vision. He could see the ground made of gold and silver, agate and lapis lazuli. But as he continued, before long there was a sudden change: the gold changed color and was transformed into a mountain of excrement. The paradisiacal scene he had worked so hard to produce was soon covered over with muck. His land of beauty was too hideous to look upon. He earnestly tried to visualize the Lord Amida, and in time his radiant Form was revealed. But suddenly that gracious Form turned into a gigantic woman, who bared her flesh and began to do a most peculiar sort of dance.

He began to feel that the visualization of the Pure Land was quite beyond his powers and confessed this to his master. His teacher laughed heartily: "Yes, I see, I see. The thirteen-stage meditation is certainly difficult; but there are lots of other meditations that can be substituted if you find that one too hard. . . . I have it! The meditation on the sun as it declines seems just right for you! It's a practice specially devised by Lord Amida for people who still have a lot of worldly passions and can't manage the thirteen stages. You'll remember that the sun meditation, first of the thirteen, involved visualizing the sun as it set in the West, where the Pure Land is. That has proved a little difficult for you, but I'm sure you'll do well with the declining-sun meditation. It's not the sun that sinks toward the Pure Land. It can be sinking in any direction—toward the mountains or the sea, the moorlands or a river. You just imagine the sun sinking! Or it doesn't have to be the sun—it could be the new moon sinking toward the mountain peaks. In fact, it doesn't have to be the sun or the moon! Just imagine a flower, or a leaf, or anything that moves downward. This is a very easy form of meditation, and also one that seems suited to you."

He did feel somehow drawn to this declining-sun meditation his master had introduced. He felt it would suit him.

And indeed the declining-sun meditation did suit him. Following his teacher's instructions, he meditated each day on the setting sun—or rather, on anything that fell or drifted downwards. Countless evening suns went down slowly, or rapidly, within his mind. And it was not only suns that dropped downwards but moons and stars, flowers and leaves, men and women. Among the men and women were his father and mother, long dead, and the wife who had left him. But as he kept on with his meditations, the falling objects and persons were replaced for some reason by the slim crescent of the new moon. After a month of meditative practice, his heart was quite purified of passions, and he could see the setting crescent moon whenever he wished. At such times, he always felt the autumn wind blowing against his skin. He reported his completion of the declining-sun meditation to his master, who rejoiced, telling him, "Your meditation is completed. I'm sure your practice will lead you to rebirth in Paradise. There's nothing more for me to teach you, and I myself would like to go to the Pure Land as soon as possible. At any rate, let's say goodbye for now."

His master now bestowed on him the religious name Rakujitsu Shufū-bō, which means "Setting Sun and Autumn Wind." Then four or five days later, the teacher again paid a visit and announced that he was going to be reborn in Paradise, and he hoped Shufū-bō would come to witness the event. Telling his disciple to follow, he set off into the Western Hills outside the capital, an area he often used to stroll in, as if it were his private garden. They had walked perhaps two hours when they came to a cliff jutting out to the east, and beneath its sharp drop was a small forest. The master had apparently chosen the spot well in advance.

"This place is due west of the capital. The sun goes down here—it's the direction of the Pure Land. If I die here, I'll be sure to go straight to Paradise. I can already see Lord Amida's gentle, smiling face. . . . Well, I'll be going then. And you should come along soon yourself!" Turning for a moment to look at his disciple, the master leapt from the top of the cliff. It happened in an instant. As the disciple stood looking down from the cliff in amazement, he saw his master's body fall like the setting crescent moon he had meditated upon so often, finally to disappear into the forest. What a sudden end! And, although a man had most certainly vanished from the world just then, the world was strangely silent, as if nothing at all had happened. Had his master really gone to the Pure Land of Perfect Bliss? Was this cliff, this valley truly the gateway to Paradise? It didn't seem so to him; and the lonely look on his master's face when he turned to gaze at him for the last time was something he could never forget.

And so it was that he had become the monk Rakujitsu Shufū-bō, leading a solitary life in retirement at Sagano. He had no intention of making the dramatic sort of exit from life that his master had. He wanted to die naturally, quietly sinking like the setting sun. So he continued his meditation on the sun and tried little by little to lose his desire to live, decreasing the amount of food he took each day, engaging in no activities, just patiently waiting for death. It was then early summer, and he was passing his days in peaceful contentment, trusting that, true to the name his master had given him, by the time the autumn winds began to blow, his life would come to an end like the sun setting in the west, and he would be able to welcome the darkness of night.

Then suddenly one day there came an intruder into Shufū-bō's quiet life. He was deep in meditation, his ego almost lost in trance, when he became aware that someone was with him. Turning around, he saw a figure standing there bearing a large cloth sack on its head.

"It's raining cats and dogs out there! The sun was shining so nicely, and now suddenly it's a downpour. I'm drenched. . . . What a mess! Lucky for me there's this hermitage out here. Excuse me, reverend sir, but I'd like to come in for a bit."

The voice was a loud one, and it belonged to a woman looking somewhat over sixty, dressed as a nun. Her face was deeply wrinkled, but she still had a womanly plumpness, and her voice was loud and lively, like a young woman's. Her eyes traveling over his modest room, she exclaimed, "My, what a shabby place! The paper screens and windows are full of holes. And there's really nothing you could call furniture. It's so bad one almost wants to applaud. You're quite the monk." She shot an upward glance at him. "Living here all alone? Why did you pick such a lonesome spot? And you still so young! You must have had some hard times. I bet some woman deceived you, you poor thing. . . ."

He had spent the last thirty days immersed in meditation without once seeing anyone, and now he felt very grateful for the presence of another human being, even if it was an old woman. He felt like talking to her, but it was not easy to get a word in as the woman jabbered on, apparently endlessly, in a loud voice. The woman completely ignored his attempts to say a word, and just kept on talking.

"My robe's all wet. I'll just have to change it. But, you know, no matter how old she gets, a woman is still a woman! You mustn't peek when a lady's changing her clothes! There's only this one room, though, isn't there? Well, just look the other way for a minute, won't you? I wouldn't want you to see me naked," she concluded with a titter.

There was nothing for it but to turn away and close his eyes, he decided; but his heart began to beat faster. The sound the cloth made as the woman took off her robe aroused thoughts of pleasure. Come to think of it, he had not touched a woman for well over ten years.

"I'm all changed. You can look now."

A flirtatious something in the woman's voice cast its spell

as he hung her wet robe on the clothes frame, one of the few furnishings in the house.

"Why, thank you. You're so kind! I see the rain's letting up. I wonder, though, if you wouldn't let me stay just a little longer, until my robe dries out. And look at this! My sack is wet right through! All my wares will be ruined. . . . Oh, this sack? It's no ordinary one, I'll tell you. It's full of treasures—rare objects that even the grandest people are eager to get hold of. I keep them in this dirty old sack to fool would-be robbers. No one would imagine a sack like this contained any treasures. Or that a woman like me would be carrying any!" She laughed again, loudly. "Do you want to take a look? I bet you do! Come a little closer, and I'll show you. I had a very good day today until the rain started. I sold an ornamental hairpin at the mansion of a Grand Councilor. It was a rare one, brought all the way from China, the finest quality item, of tortoise shell worked with gold and silver. The Grand Councilor's wife loved it the minute she saw it, and snapped it up. And oh yes . . . I have another one very like it right here. I'll show it to you." The woman removed from her wretched, filthy-looking sack a fine tortoise shell hairpin. "Nice, isn't it? Its price is twenty *ryō*. I sold it to the lady for fifteen. You think I lost five *ryō* on the deal? Don't be silly, I *made* five *ryō*, because I bought it for ten! The lady is awfully tight-fisted; she never buys anything at the asking-price. So today I pushed for thirty *ryō* right off. I knew she wanted it; she *had* to have it. But 'Too high,' she says. 'Make it cheaper.' So I said, 'This hairpin could suit only a person of quality like your ladyship. I'm honored if it pleases you. So I'll give it to you for half-price, just fifteen *ryō*.' She was very pleased: 'Oh, thank you! It's nice of you to come down so much.' As she thanked me, she handed right over the fifteen *ryō* in cash. I made five *ryō* and got thanked into the bargain—what more could I ask for? I'm good at business, don't you think? Anyway, I'd made my five *ryō* so I closed up shop for the day. I was hurrying to get home when this rain started. I don't know whether you'd call it good luck or bad. I guess I'd have to say good, since that's how I met you!"

The shower had ended, and the room was now wrapped in darkness. "Well, I'll have to be on my way now. Thanks for everything. I'd like to give you a little present for sheltering me from the rain like this. Let's see. . . . Oh, yes. There's this little wooden drum. The one you have is so shabby-looking! This is a good one. Here, take it. It's a really fine piece, from a famous temple. I don't mind parting with it, if you'll make use of it." Drawing from her sack the fish-shaped wooden drum, she gave it a few taps. It was indeed a fine drum, in its heart-piercing beauty of tone even more than in its outward shape.

"Isn't that a fine sound? Here, you try it out." He did as he was told. It *was* a good sound, but one that seemed out of keeping with his modest hermitage. "Never mind, never mind, just take it. And I'll take this old drum of yours along with me." Without waiting for a yes or no, the woman exchanged the old drum for the new, and, as if some new and urgent work awaited her, stuffed the old drum along with her now-dry robe into the sack. "I may be back some time," she said without turning to look at him, and was off.

Just who was she? the man wondered. It was natural for her to seek shelter from the rain, but what was she doing out here in the outskirts of the capital to begin with? Was there really a nobleman's villa somewhere nearby? Even so, it was a wonder that she'd stumbled on his little hut. . . . He couldn't get the mysterious old nun out of his mind. He had had nothing to do with others for a long time now. Thirty days ago a villager had brought him a little rice and salt and bean-paste, but he never had long, friendly talks even with the villager. The first real human contact he had had since his master's death was his encounter today with the old woman.

His only friends for a great while had been the setting sun and the autumn wind; but now a woman—aged to be sure, but still a woman—had invaded his solitude. More than that, she had stridden roughshod into his heart. He knew that he was handling the whole matter very badly, and regretted it; but there was no denying that the woman's warm, frank ways had disturbed his heart, which had up till now been set solely on the Pure Land.

It was ten days later that the woman suddenly appeared again. Just as before, she chattered away for some time and then hurried off. From then on she visited him often and asked lots of questions about his personal affairs. He, however, refused to say a word about his past. She told him everything about herself: she was, she said, of noble birth, had been married but lost her husband, and so became a nun. She'd been quite attractive in her youth and had had lots of admirers, but had always strictly protected her chastity. He couldn't tell if all this was true or a pack of lies. Some of what she said seemed clearly false; actually, though, he couldn't have cared less if what she said about herself was accurate or not. Why should he care about the old woman's past or present, when he himself was aiming at rebirth in the Pure Land in the near future?

Each time she came to visit, the woman brought various foods for him—rice, vegetables, fruit, and even at times venison. "I suppose you'll say you can't eat this meat because you're a monk. But didn't the famous St. Shinran himself say that a monk can eat meat, or even have a wife? Don't be such a stick-in-the-mud—it's delicious meat! Have a good feed. It'll build you up, give you some energy. You're still a young man!"

As he looked at the venison she had taken care to leave, he couldn't help laughing. He'd grown rather plump recently, gorging himself on whatever food she left, whether rice or vegetables or fruit. It was a far cry from his earlier plans to reduce his daily food until he eventually starved to death. Yet the contrast between his past ideals and present practice did not depress him. In fact, it made him laugh. And so, in the end, he polished off even the venison the woman had left behind.

However, he knew in his heart that this would have to stop. "The next time she comes, I'll just refuse: 'Get out and don't come back!' I'll say." He often told himself this, as he ate his meat and rice. Yet it was also true that the woman's kindness had come to mean a great deal to him. And so the days passed, with him never quite able to send her on her way.

He attempted to purify his mind by performing the declining-sun meditation, but the familiar image of the sun sinking until it became a slim crescent like the new moon no longer appeared. He no longer heard the sound of the autumn wind. Instead, the crescent-shaped setting sun grew bigger and bigger day by day (like his own body) until it turned into the red globe of the sun at noon. The autumn wind vanished, and in its place a soft spring breeze bore the sweet scent of flowers.

One day the woman came by carrying a big pumpkin on her head. As always, she kept up a constant stream of talk; and then, on the point of leaving, she said, "You know, the single life is all very well, but there's also something to be said for living as a twosome. You've got some color in your cheeks now; you look a lot healthier. So how about it? Wouldn't you like to take a wife? After all, you say you've completed your preparations for going to Paradise, but if you die, somebody'll have to give you a funeral. And that's a wife's job. You think you can just die on your own? It's not so easy nowadays, I'm afraid. No, you'll need somebody, and that somebody might as well be your wife. So why don't you get married?

"I have somebody in mind for you. She's the daughter of a noble family that's fallen on hard times; her father died recently, and she has no one now. She's in her mid-twenties—a little old for a bride maybe, but it's because she was such a good daughter. Her mother never was very well, and she looked after her for so many years that she passed her prime. Then, after her mother died, she had to take care of her father, and she did a really good job of it, too. She was a filial daughter all right, but so unfortunate! An only child, lost both her parents, and now all alone in the world. . . . And she'll do whatever I say. . . . Her looks? Oh, she's a beauty, she is—nice, full figure. And she's a virgin to boot! You'll never find another one like her. So marry her. She'll make you a fine bride.

"She must be joking, you're thinking to yourself. Would any woman want to come live in this miserable little monk's hut? you're about to ask. Well, she would, I tell you. The truth is, I've already spoken about the matter to the girl herself. And she said that if there were someone who'd care for her, she'd be happy to marry him and try to be the best little wife she possibly could. Far better than remaining a spinster all her life, she said. Now wasn't that a splendid answer? I know she'll be a hard worker; and then, after you pass away, she'll give you a wonderful funeral and make sure you rest in peace.

"All right, then, it's settled. Of course there's a bit of a gap in age, but that won't matter once you've lived together for a while. I'll go and make all the arrangements, so you just wait here."

The woman hurried off, leaving the pumpkin on the veranda. He didn't really put much faith in this sudden talk of a bride, but nonetheless it made him feel a bit uneasy. He was too upset, in fact, to bother with the pumpkin, which remained where it was on the veranda.

He was falling in love, in love with the girl of noble family the old woman had described to him, the dutiful daughter he was still to meet. It was not that he had never known a woman before; he had had quite enough of them. Yet now, for some reason, despite his years, he felt his heart throbbing with a new emotion. His imagination knew no bounds; as he did his meditation, the naked body of this girl he had not seen would appear before him. He was sure that, indulging in such lewd thoughts, he would fall into the Hell-Forest-with-Leaves-that-Cut-Like-Swords of which his master had warned him. In that particular hell, the condemned sinner would see a beautiful woman perched at the top of a tree. It would be a woman from his past, and she would beckon to him, calling "Come to me, come to me." The man, unable to restrain himself, would try to climb the tree, and each leaf would turn into a sword and pierce his flesh. Without doubt, he would fall into that hell—or rather, he had already fallen into it.

But was this not what men meant by "love"? He was in anguish, and he waited impatiently for the old woman's return.

And yet, though she had been such a frequent visitor in the past, ever since that day's conversation the woman had stopped coming. So, she had just been teasing him after all . . . But his mind would not return to its former calm. He *had* to see the woman once more. Yet he didn't even know her name. How would he ever find her?

Perhaps two months had passed, and the autumn winds had begun to blow when she appeared. "What a lovely season, and how beautiful the *susuki* grasses are! You're rather like a fox living in a field of *susuki,* so we'll have a 'foxes' wedding,' like in the old stories! No, no, I'm just joking. The girl's no fox-spirit, you needn't worry about that.

"If I'm a little late with the preparations it's because the girl's so filial. 'I should remain single and devote the rest of my life to prayer for my parents' souls,' she says—even though she *is* interested, I know. But she's such a dutiful daughter! Well, I worked at her day in and day out, pointing out how her parents would be looking down from heaven, pleased as could be at her making a happy marriage. I wasn't forcing her, mind you. I knew she wanted to. Anyway, she agreed to marry you at one point; but then, well, they may have come down in the world, but she is from a very good family, you know, and she was worried about what people would say. And she didn't want to be seen as 'easy'. But I said, 'Try to see it from my point of view. Your dear dead parents specially asked me to look after you. Besides, you can't devote your whole life to the dead. No, dear, the best thing for a woman is to find a man who loves her, and marry him. This is a god-send for you!' Well, she just bent her head, blushed, and said in a quiet little voice, 'Yes, I understand. Thank you for all you've done for me.' She's a good girl.

"So I arranged to have her come here exactly ten days from now. I suppose I could bring her myself; but she's so bashful, somehow I think she'd be more comfortable coming on her own. That'd be all right, wouldn't it?

"But can't we do something about this room of yours? You need at least some furniture and fittings to welcome your new bride. Oh, and first of all, there's the bedding to think about. You can't spend your bridal night on these paper-thin futon of yours. I'll give you a new set of futon as a wedding-present, how's that? On the other hand, futon *are* awfully dear. . . . Let's go half and half on it! Leading the pious life you do, you can hardly have much need for money. Just let me have what you've got here now."

The woman had, on her frequent visits to the little hut, taken a good look 'round and knew very well that he had a little money tucked away somewhere. He took out a one *ryō* piece and placed it in front of her.

"Ahh, so you *do* have some money! One *ryō*—wonderful!"

That single *ryō* had been meant for his funeral expenses.

"We can buy some fine nuptial bedding with this!" The woman trotted off with the money in hand. The next day, a fine, thick futon of a sort that he had never slept on, or even seen, was delivered to the hermitage. The splendid bedding seemed quite out of place in his shabby dwelling. He set to work at once on repairs, patching the holes in the roof and putting new paper in the screens and windows. The little hut came to life—it was almost unrecognizable. The bright red futon was placed in the center of the room, and it felt as if the girl herself had already arrived. Gazing at the soft red futon, he imagined his wedding night.

The day before the girl was due to come, the old woman appeared again. "My, what a difference! The room's nice and clean, and how warm that futon looks. It'll play its part in the most important ceremony of all. You haven't had any practice in that for quite some time, have you? Well, do your best. And remember, she's a virgin, so be very, very gentle. All right then, I'll be sending her along tomorrow night."

The day itself had come at last. In his mind there was no longer a trace of the crescent-shaped setting sun or the sound of the autumn wind. All he could envision was the figure of the girl. Then suddenly he became uneasy. He had not touched a woman for over ten years, and he was not quite sure he would know how to make love to his bride. He had a drink, and then another, and then a third, until at last he was very, very drunk. Sleep overcame him, and everything that had happened to him seemed like no more than a dream. Waking from sleep, he found that the sun had set, and it was completely dark.

There was a sound. The girl must have arrived!

"What's this? The bedding isn't even spread out." It was the woman's voice.

"And you, you're drunk! I was worried so I came on over to see how the preparations for the wedding night were getting on. It's a good thing I did."

Unrolling the bedding, she urged him to "give it his best," and turned out the light before leaving. "And don't turn the light on; she's a shy little thing." These last words rang through the darkened room, and she was gone. No sooner had she left than he became aware of someone else's presence. So she had come at last! A robe that even in the darkness was obviously red covered her from head to toe. The room was suffused with a feeling of girlish high-spirits.

"How do you do, sir? I am very pleased to meet you," she said in a high voice. It sounded somehow familiar; but he made his own formal greeting in the usual way. Then the bride and groom performed the ritual exchange of cups of saké, as the woman had said they should; and, that ended, the groom placed his bride beneath the crimson quilt. He drew her close. Her flesh was softer and fuller even than the bridal quilts, but her hands and feet seemed rather rough and dry. What worried him, though, was whether or not he would be able to acquit himself well during the next, all-important ritual. It was easier than he had thought, and he was able to bring the marriage rites to a happy conclusion. Perhaps from relief, and certainly with the help of all the saké he had drunk, he slept soundly till morning.

The rays of the morning sun struck his face and he opened

his eyes, dazzled. There, lying beside him was—could it be?—the old woman! He was too amazed to speak. The woman turned to him, with a long, loud guffaw: "Surprised? But you were nice and gentle last night. I'll be a good wife to you. I may be a bit on in years, but as we spend time together, you'll care less and less about that. The most important thing is that we like each other. I liked you from the very first moment—that's why I kept visiting you. And you didn't exactly dislike me either, I'd say. I'm an old hand at business, so putting food into your mouth will be no problem at all. So, I'm an ideal wife! Ha, ha, ha, ha." And again she laughed, very loudly indeed, and with a look of great satisfaction. The man himself looked as if he had been tricked by a fox-spirit.

"We'll have a long and happy life together! This sack of mine is full of treasures. I'll be your 'god of good fortune'."

The man's mouth was open, but he said nothing as he listened to the woman's words. Finally he roused himself to say, "Tell me your name."

"Oyō. I'm out to be of service (go-yō) to everyone, so they called me the 'go-yō nun' as I went about selling things. Then 'go-yō' somehow became 'o-yō,' and now everybody calls me the Nun Oyō."

"Oyō. . . ." He murmured the woman's name and wondered if perhaps he had not always known in some corner of his heart that the girl that Oyō had promised to introduce would turn out to be, in fact, Oyō herself.

A Tale of Luck and Riches

Near Seventh Avenue in Kyoto an old couple lived a wretched life in one of ten linked tenement apartments. It was close to the end of autumn, and from the cracks in the door a cold wind came blowing in. It was still evening, but the old man and woman had rolled themselves into their thin quilts for warmth and were having a talk:

"The cold chills you through. If it's like this now, just think how it'll be when winter comes. How are we going to get through it? We don't have any coal or rice."

"Oh, it'll work out somehow. Even if we don't have anything, we'll manage to survive. We've scraped by up to now, haven't we?"

"You've been talking like that for forty years now, just lazing your days away."

"I haven't been lazy. You know very well that when I was young, I tried my hand at lots of things. But nothing worked out—like there was some kind of evil plague-spirit that had got its claws into me. Well, if I'm going to fail at everything

I do, I might just as well do nothing at all, I said to myself. I decided to take it easy."

"That's fine for you, but it makes things awfully hard for me, you know. Nothing good to eat, no decent clothes to wear, having to live in an old tenement like this. Yes, there must be a plague-spirit attached to you.... Or you yourself are a plague-spirit. Poor me, having hooked myself up with something like that!"

"So now you're calling me a plague-spirit, are you?"

"I am indeed. If you don't like it, then try getting rid of that evil spirit, the one that's been part of you for these past forty years, until it's *become* you—try getting rid of *that!*"

"What a way to talk! And anyway, I sure would get rid of it if only I could.... But what can I do?"

"You should go pray to the roadside god on Fifth Avenue. He's a very powerful god, they say, and he tells people what kind of work is right for them. Heisuke was told to start a greengrocer's, and he made a fortune. The god told Professor Chikurin to take to robbery, and now he's the best-known brigand in the whole capital."

"Ahh, I don't put any faith in divine oracles. It's just a way for the priests to rake in the money."

"It's no wonder you're under a curse, saying things like that. Go and ask the god's advice, anyway. What have you got to lose?"

"Ahh, I don't feel like doing it."

"What a shilly-shallier you are! I'm sick to death of you. Will you listen to me for a change, just this once? Go and ask. It'll bring you good luck."

With his wife continually at him that way, the old man could hardly fail to do something. Unwillingly, he dragged himself to his feet, changed into streetwear, and betook himself to Tenjin Woods near Fifth Avenue, to receive the deity's oracle. Strange to say, the mere act of going to the shrine seemed to arouse some pious feeling in the old man. He prayed earnestly to the god to "please tell me the kind of work I should do," and, after a short time, a priest emerged and handed him a twig: "I asked the god about the right kind of work for you. The answer was that you are a person of exceptional spiritual powers, and the god will give you direction privately, in a dream. This twig is from a seven-leaved *nanten* bush. Place it under your pillow before you go to sleep on the night of the winter solstice. On toward dawn, you'll see a dream in which the will of the god for you will be revealed."

Now the old man had never had much faith in religion, and he suspected the priest was just making it all up; yet a certain curiosity quickened his footsteps as he made his way home. Arriving back, he told his wife exactly what the priest had said. She was a believer, devoted to the gods and inclined to trust whatever oracles came her way, so she was all a-twitter. "The winter solstice is only a few days off, and then the god himself will tell you what job to take to change our bad luck into good!" All her hopes were set upon the promised dream.

The night of the solstice came round. The old woman used every penny she had to buy saké and special foods. Her husband ate and drank his fill (it was for the first time in a great while), and then went to bed happy. His wife had been much kinder to him than usual.

Next morning, when the old man woke up, his wife asked eagerly if he had had a dream. He was not the sort of man who dreams very often; and, though he had carefully placed the *nanten* twig under his pillow, it seemed that last night too he had failed to dream. But his wife kept after him until at last, straining to remember, he began to feel vaguely that he might have had some sort of dream on toward dawn. He dredged the depths of his memory for the remnants of that dream.

"A mandarin orange (mikan) . . . I saw something like a mandarin orange. But it was also sort of like an iron bell. Then I seem to remember hearing a pleasant sound. Oh, of course, it was the jingling of the bell! It was a fine sound."

"A funny dream. I can't make out what it means. Surely the god isn't telling you to go into the mandarin orange business—or the iron or the bell business either, for that matter."

No matter how hard they tried, the old couple couldn't make head or tail of the dream. Then the old woman had an idea: "I've got it! There's a man named Abe Hayasuke, known throughout the city for interpreting dreams. You should go and see him. They say he never misses!"

So the two of them went off and knocked on Abe Hayasuke's door. His house was crowded with people come to ask the meaning of their dreams. When, after a considerable wait, their turn came, Hayasuke appeared to take no notice of their wretched clothes and greeted them with the words "Well now, sir, what sort of dream have you seen?" The old woman explained about the oracle of the wayside god and the dream; and the dream-reader thought for a bit before beginning to speak: "A most unusual message from the gods. No one in all Japan has ever before received such an oracle! Now this is what it means: *mikan*, or *mikara*— 'from one's person.' From one's person, there comes an iron bell, with a very nice sound. Well, obviously, that's means breaking wind! The dream is telling you to break wind in a melodious way—turn it into an art, and you'll be a rich man in no time. Remember, another word for iron is *kane*, and that also means 'money.' So it's a very lucky dream, promising plenty of money for you, my friend."

The old couple sat there for a time, dazed at Hayasuke's

unexpected reading of the dream. Suddenly, though, the old woman spoke up, as if remembering something: "He's hopeless, he is, fails at everything he does—why, we've been lucky to survive this long. But at least his farts are good and loud. . . . I've thought it strange all these years. . . . And they're not just loud, they've a fine sound to them, and they go on and on. It's often I said to myself, 'Ah, if only the man was as fine as his farts are!' Yes, I well remember thinking that."

Then Hayasuke said, as if he too were drawing on old memories, "The Way of Wind-breaking is one of the Forty-eight Arts going back as far as Prince Shōtoku himself. I remember when I was a child there was still one man proficient in the art who gave public concerts down by the Kamo River. I thought all that was gone forever, but now the god is urging you to restore the splendid lost Art of Wind-breaking. What great good fortune for us all!"

The old woman was happy as could be. "Oh, thank you so much, dear Mr. Abe. I don't know how to express our gratitude. We're very poor, you see, and can't really give you the fee you deserve."

"Don't worry about that. You can pay me after you've gotten rich—or not at all, as you like," replied the dream-reader. "But do me the favor of letting me hear one good blast right here and now—how about it?"

The old woman chimed in at once: "Yes, let's hear one of your finest. Come on, now, out with it."

The old man, willing to oblige, rolled up the skirt of his kimono to expose his rear, got down on all fours, summoned all his strength, and farted. High and lovely was the sound! To their ears, it sounded like "Pp-pp, patterned robes. Bb-bb, brocades. Jj-jj, jingling gold." Hearing it, Hayasuke said with great dignity and formality, "A truly wondrous sound. I warrant it will be the talk of the capital."

The old couple returned home overcome at the prospect of such unlooked-for good fortune. The old man wanted the very next day to give a performance of that art in which, as Hayasuke had assured him, the cultivated people of the capital would delight. His wife, however, was more cautious. "Of course it's a fine sound as it is, but you're a little lacking in variety. Leave it that way, and I'm afraid your artistic career will be short." This was the old woman's firm opinion, and so she made her husband practice long and hard, giving him very specific directions as to crescendos, diminuendos, sostenutos, and the like.

Now the old woman was very fond of the works of the Noh master Zeami, who had divided the Art of the Noh into three general styles: the August Style, the Martial Style, and the Feminine Style. She decided to try to perfect her husband's Art along the lines of Zeami's theories. The August Style would be used for the crepitations of a god, or other venerable personage. The Martial Style was for samurai (or, more generally, masculine) farts. And the Feminine Style was reserved for breaking of wind on the part of young ladies. Divine crepitation would have to be somewhat reserved and ethereal; a man's farts, vigorous and forceful; and a lady's wind, soft and delicate. The old woman insisted that her husband learn clearly to distinguish these three styles in performance. She then went on to compose numerous "pieces for wind instrument," all based on Zeami's Three Styles. The old man's progress was rapid, and within three months he could do justice to even the most taxing composition. In the fourth month, his wife took him along to the shrine of the wayside god and offered prayers for the success of his first public concert.

Shortly afterwards a strange rumor began to spread throughout the capital: "They say there's going to be a wind concert soon on Suzaku Avenue." "Apparently there's this master farter named Takamuku Hidetake—he's going to give the most extraordinary performance." Soon the people of the capital were informed of the actual date of the wind concert.

"Lovers of novelty are the people of the capital," as the old saying goes, and indeed there was a great crowd of onlookers on Suzaku Avenue at the appointed day and hour. The old couple appeared, the woman dressed like a Shinto priestess and the man in courtier's costume of the previous age (which created a rather comical effect). After the woman had delivered an impressive-sounding introduction, her husband began to dance, waggling his buttocks before the intent gaze of the audience. "Aya-chū-chū, nishiki-sara-sara, goyō-no-matsubara, toppin-parapin-no-pppuuu!"

It was undeniably the sound of breaking wind, yet it hardly seemed so to any in the audience. It had such beauty of tone, it seemed variously like the soughing of the wind in some shadowy valley, or the twitterings of birds, or the deep roll of a drum. The audience was overcome with amazement, half shocked, half entranced by the sound. When at last the concert was over, there was wave upon wave of applause. In their excitement, the crowd flung at the great master of wind-breaking Takamuku Hidetake and his wife everything they had—the fans they held in their hands, the clothes on their backs, and the money in their purses. The old man and woman bowed deeply to the audience, looking rather awkward as they did so, picked up the offerings, and hurried off. The crowd was still so excited that it seemed unwilling to leave the spot.

Thus, all of Kyoto was soon talking about "the old farter," as some termed him. But his wife was still very cautious. It would not do for her husband to give these concerts every day. No, he would have to rest for several days, concentrating his energies and re-tuning. The first concert on Suzaku

Avenue had been on the day of the ox, and so the second was set for the day of the horse, six days later.

Each time a concert was given on Suzaku Avenue, the audience grew, as did the volume of applause and the amount of gold and other valuables with which the old couple were showered. Then one day a messenger came from a lieutenant general of the guards who lived on Imadegawa, asking for a wind concert at the gentleman's residence on a certain day and time. Now the lieutenant general was a nobleman who enjoyed the Emperor's favor and a man of culture versed in music, dance, and all the arts. And here he was, eager to hear the old man break wind! The couple were ecstatic and prepared themselves for the great day with even more intense practice.

The concert turned out to be a great success. Apart from the lieutenant general himself, there was a large number of noblemen with a personal interest in music and dance gathered there. Grand Councilors and Middle Councilors alike waited with keen anticipation to see just what kind of concert would be given by this man famed throughout the town as "the old farter." Especially numerous in the audience were the ladies of the court, who had heard rumors of the old farter's existence and were wild to hear and see him. Yet they couldn't bring themselves to be so shameless as to sneak out of the palace and make their way to Suzaku Avenue to listen, in public, to the sound of farting. Thus, when a message came from the lieutenant general, inviting them to his residence for a private concert, they vied with one another in their haste to accept and, taking along their closest friends, rushed off to Imadegawa.

The couple made their entrance in the usual formal costumes and, after an impressive introduction by the old woman, the husband began to dance. "Goyō-no-matsubara, toppin-pararin-no-pppuuu." The ladies had hidden themselves behind folding screens and were trying to keep from laughing; but soon they could hold back no longer, and began to giggle. The laughter spread from one to the other, like an epidemic; and by the time the performance ended, there were gales of shameless mirth. One of the court ladies actually rolled about on the floor; while another laughed so hard that she began to choke, and only a timely cup of water saved her.

The lieutenant general was extremely pleased and gave various presents to the couple. The courtiers, too, and the nobility from Grand Councilors on down showered them with possessions. The old couple had brought along a boy to help carry the gifts they anticipated receiving; but what they actually got weighed far too much for even the three of them to carry off.

The concert at the lieutenant general's house solidified Takamuku Hidetake's fame, making him a much-talked-about figure not only in the market-place but even in the Imperial Palace. As a result, there were command performances one after another at the palaces of the Grand and Middle Councilors. The Emperor himself attended a concert at one of the Grand Councilors' palaces and was reported to be exceedingly pleased with what he heard—so pleased, in fact, that he bestowed the title of Master on this famous artful farter. Yet, although Takamuku Hidetake had risen so far as to be granted an audience with the Emperor and be given the official title of Master, he never neglected to perform for the general public as well. And so his popularity kept on growing, and he and his wife kept on getting richer and richer.

A full year had passed since the night when the two of them had had that momentous conversation as they lay wrapped in their meager quilts. Once again the old couple chatted with one another as they lay in bed in their section of the ten-apartment tenement. The look of their room, though, was completely different from what it had been a year before. The cracked door and broken-down screens were nowhere to be seen. The door now displayed a splendid painting on its surface, while the sliding screens were of thick, Chinese-style paper covered with silver- and gold-leaf. The old couple no longer slept on wafer-thin quilts, but on layer upon layer of thick silken bedding, far more than was necessary to merely fend off the cold. All around were ranged the gifts they had received, covering the floor from wall to wall till there was hardly room left for the two of them.

"You know, it's a whole year since that day you went to pray to the wayside god. Time flies, doesn't it."

"Only a year? It feels like much longer ago. One year, and our life has changed totally!"

And indeed, that single year had wrought great changes for them—above all, in the fact that a year before they had been so poor they did not know if they would survive the winter, but now they were so famous that everyone in the capital knew their names, and they had become very rich. The old woman even *looked* different. No doubt because of the good food she was getting, she had put some meat on her bones, grown plump, and looked ten years younger. The old man, on the other hand, had not changed a bit; he was as thin as ever. If he ate too much rich food, his art suffered, so he had to exercise continual restraint. Even so, his face shone with a new happiness. He was no longer a miserable old man eking out his wretched life; the rigors of dedication to his art lent a special radiance to his face and filled his body with new energy.

"I'm grateful to you, because if you hadn't urged me to go and pray that day, my luck would never have changed."

"That's right. *I* changed your luck. But I could only do it because you had that special talent right from the start. I just helped you uncover it."

"It's not talent so much as luck. Anyone could master this art."

"What are you saying? Why, your belly, your rear-end, they're one in ten thousand—no, one in a hundred thousand!"

"That's not true. Sometimes I think all this must be a dream, and that we'll wake up one of these days. My art's . . . not worth a fart! Anybody could learn it, that's what I think."

"Don't be so weak-spirited! You want to lose everything we've built up? No—we have to protect what we've got!"

"I won't be able to protect it. The god giveth and the god taketh away."

"Look, the god gave you this good fortune, but now that it's come your way, it's *your* job to hang on to it and not let it get away. That's what the god wants. And if anybody tries to take it away from you, he'll have me to deal with!"

The old woman insisted that her husband guard his present position whatever happened, and said she'd allow no one to threaten it. Jumping out of bed, she took something from a chest of drawers. "If anyone does come along and cause problems, just give him some of this," she commanded, handing her husband two medicinal pellets.

Now unbeknownst to them, this exchange was overheard by a third party, the wife of their next door neighbor, one Fukutomi Oribe. Fukutomi (whose name meant "Luck-and-Riches") was as poor a man as Takamuku Hidetake had ever been. In his youth he had inexplicably fallen in love with and married a woman ten years older than himself, and ugly. Thus, though he was ten years younger than Hidetake, his wife was older than their neighbor. This woman had a bald patch toward the center of her scalp. Her eyes slanted sharply upward at the corners and were, in addition, asymmetrically placed. Her mouth split off at the corners in the direction of either ear. The people of the area generally referred to her as "the old witch." But husband and wife got along extremely well. They were very poor but had one consolation: that next to them lived the old couple who were even poorer than themselves. Every time they complained of their own poverty, they concluded with the comforting remark, "We're better off than *they* are, anyway." Now, suddenly, the next-door neighbors were very rich; they had robbed the Fukutomis of the single greatest consolation in their dismal lives.

"Filthy rich they are now, those two old fools! There's no reason we can't be the same," thought the old witch. And so, saying nothing to her husband, she had gone over to spy on them. She had not managed to hear everything that was said, but she clearly recalled the old man stating that anyone could master the art of farting and that he'd surely lose his position to somebody someday. She rushed back home and said to her husband, "You know that arty farting the old fool next door engages in? Well, I *know* that you can do it too! Imagine the two of them trying to monopolize it, and making a pile of money in the process! Oh, it makes me sick, just sick to think of it!"

"But the art of farting is not such a simple thing to learn."

"You're wrong. I heard it with my own ears: anybody can do it."

"You mean, I could do it too?"

"Sure you could. If that fool can do it, why can't you? You're younger than he is, and your farts'll be livelier than anything that dried-up old thing can produce. You'll replace him in no time."

"Hmm. I wonder. . . I'd sure like to."

"And you will, you will! You'll master the art of farting

and become the most famous artist in the capital. We'll be rich, no question about it."

"Shall I give it a try, then?"

"Of course. You'll be the world's champion farter, and we'll have our revenge on those two old fools next door!"

The Fukutomis had a family to support, unlike the Takamukus next door. There had been many children, and the eldest son had married early, but after the birth of his first child the son had fallen ill and died (partly for lack of money to take proper care of him). The Fukutomis' other children had all married and settled down by then, but they were left with the care of the young widow and her child, not yet four. Fukutomi now had to try to support his wife, daughter-in-law, and grandchild all on his own. He himself had not much minded the success of his next-door neighbors, but, egged on by the old witch, he began to feel that for the sake of his daughter-in-law and her child he ought indeed to learn the art of farting from his neighbor and try to rise in the world. However, he felt embarrassed to ask, in the name of neighborliness, to become the pupil of a man whom he had up to then treated with considerable contempt, and so he kept on postponing the request.

In the meantime, the now wealthy couple next door had moved to a fine new house on Fifth Avenue where it rises into the eastern hills. One reason for the move was that it would not do for an artist who had received the title of Master from the Emperor to live in a shabby, broken-down tenement. An even more important reason was to escape from the jealous, envious eyes of their fellow tenement dwellers. Now that they had suddenly struck it rich, the neighbors who had hitherto completely ignored them, or showed outright contempt, underwent a change in attitude that was total. Some people now approached them as if they had always been the closest of friends and offered humble flattery. Some declared that it was a great honor for the whole tenement that it had produced such eminent persons. There were, alas, also evil-doers who crept into the couple's room while they were gone in order to relieve them of some of their now too-abundant treasures. (There was a certain congruity between this last group and those who were so generous in their praise.) And so there grew about the couple a circle of fawning flatterers; but those who could not hope to enter that circle and enjoy its benefits felt hatred for their more adept neighbors and soon began to revile the old couple who had caused all the fuss as villains of the worst sort. It was this kind of trouble with their neighbors that the Takamukus wanted to escape.

After the couple had moved away, the old witch went at her husband: "You and all your dithering! Now get on over to their new house." She made such a racket about it that even the always slow-to-act Fukutomi was galvanized into action.

Fifth Avenue at the eastern hills. The Takamuku residence was even grander than rumor suggested. There were so many gates, one was at a loss where to enter. Fortunately, just then a servant emerged from the mansion, so Fukutomi gave his name and asked to be announced. Very soon Hidetake himself appeared, courteously inviting his former neighbor to come in. Relieved to find Hidetake as modest and friendly as always, Fukutomi sped through his formal greetings and then blurted out his request: "I hope you'll accept me as student and teach me the art of farting."

"There's no need to learn it specially—anybody can do it."

"But there must be some knack, some special technique . . ."

Since the other was so insistent, Hidetake agreed to teach him the secrets of the art. Fukutomi went to Hidetake's house for lessons a number of times, and the Master gladly taught him the essentials of farting, showing great kindness and patience in the process.

One day, after the lesson, the Master quietly began: "I have nothing more to teach you. You've mastered it all. Now just give me a brief demonstration of what you've learned." Whereupon Fukutomi bared his buttocks, got down on all fours, gathered all his strength in his belly, and let fly: "Pppuuu."

Hidetake thought for a bit: "It's a fine sound. Yes, you're already a master farter." Then, continuing, "Now, when you give a major performance, I suggest you eat your fill of really first-class food beforehand and then take some of this medicine here. You'll find it'll improve your tone." And he gave his pupil the two pellets his wife had given him.

Fukutomi's heart was dancing, and his feet seemed barely to touch the ground as he returned home, Hidetake's parting words still ringing in his ears: "You're a professional; you are ready to perform anytime, anywhere." And when he got home and told the whole story to the old witch, her joy was even greater than his.

"You see, it's all turned out just as I said it would. You're a qualified farter. The man himself called you a professional, didn't he? But why didn't he tell you to give your debut concert on Suzaku Avenue, I wonder. Or why didn't he urge you to present yourself at the lieutenant general's residence? He must be jealous! He knows your farts are of finer quality than his own, and he's afraid you'll take away his audience. That's why he said nothing, mediocrity that he is. You're younger, and your farts are louder, livelier, better in every way. Don't bother with a concert on Suzaku Avenue—go right for the lieutenant general's. Then you'll replace him as the greatest farter in the land! Go on now, off to the lieutenant general's with you!" she cried, and Fukutomi himself began to think it not a bad idea. "So, he's jealous of me, is he? . . ." he muttered. "All right, then, I'll go to the lieutenant general's tomorrow."

What a time the two of them had that night! The old witch prepared a pile of delicacies to set before her husband. "Eat, eat," she urged. And he, thinking of the morrow, ate as much as he could. The two of them could not stop laughing as they thought of the mountain of gifts they would be getting from the lieutenant general. They'd get this, they'd get that—it was like a dream! Finally, late that night, holding his belly filled to bursting, Fukutomi went to bed.

He awoke to find his wife already up and about, with everything prepared for the big day. There was even a large cart waiting in front of the house—wherever had she found it?

"Your reward from the lieutenant general will be too heavy for you to carry. This cart should just about do, though, so take it with you when you go."

Fukutomi reached the residence a little before noon. The guard at the gate came out, looking rather severely at the man and his cart, and demanded to know his business.

"My name is Fukutomi Oribe. I am master of the art of farting as practiced by Takamuku Hidetake, who enjoys the patronage of the lieutenant general. I have come all the way from Seventh Avenue here to Imadegawa, hoping to display my art before your master." He threw out his chest and spoke impressively; and the guard, hearing the phrase "Hidetake's master," or something like it, decided he could not ignore the man and hurried to report to the lieutenant general.

"What? Hidetake's master? I've never heard of anyone like that. . . ." The officer thought it strange but had the man summoned into his presence, wishing to see for himself. Leaving his cart beside the gate, Fukutomi was escorted to the room where the officer was.

"You claim to be the teacher of Takamuku Hidetake: are you, in fact? You look perhaps ten years younger than he."

"It is true, sir, that I am ten years his junior. Yet, young as I am, I am in fact his teacher. The fellow copies my art and then ignores my existence—that's why he said nothing of me to you, sir. The man has *stolen* my art!"

"Stolen? Hidetake has? I find that hard to credit. . . . Still, since you are so positive about it, perhaps I ought to believe you. To tell the truth, I've become just a trifle bored with Hidetake's farting lately. If you are indeed his teacher, you should be able to perform even more impressively than he. Let me hear you."

Suddenly the official residence was full of bustle. While Fukutomi ate his hoped-for lunch, messengers went out to various parts of the capital—to the residences of the Grand Councilors and the Middle Councilors, and to the Imperial Palace itself. Soon the guests began to arrive—the Grand Councilors, the Middle Councilors, and, from the Palace, the court ladies in all their finery.

The residence was filled to overflowing with these noble persons. Fukutomi, having eaten his fill of the splendid lunch and taken the two pellets, was ready to go onstage. The audience waited in breathless anticipation of a demonstration of supreme artfulness. He made his entrance and began to dance: "Pppuuu." There was something a bit odd about this first blast, but the artist just gathered his strength and tried again. "Bbb. Bbb. Bbbuu. Buri-buri. Bu-bu-bu-bu."

The sound was not that of wind breaking but of loose bowels exploding. Fukutomi was surprised, of course; but thinking it was some minor problem, he gamely went on dancing and farting with all his might. He was sure that at any moment he would produce a good sound, a ravishingly fine sound. But all he did produce was a great quantity of excreta. It was as if golden snow had piled up all around, followed by rain. But the golden snow and rain gave off the most appalling odor which assaulted the noses of the fine ladies and gentlemen who filled the chamber. People scattered in all directions, seeking to escape from the stench. The lieutenant general fled to an inner room, holding his nose. Once there, he found himself laughing at the ludicrous situation; then, thinking of how the garden he took such pride in had been ruined, his anger blazed forth.

"Give the fellow a good thrashing," he commanded, and his retainers went to work with a will, beating Fukutomi mercilessly with poles. Each time he was struck, a strong smell arose from the fellow's body; and the greater the stench, the angrier his assailants became. He was soon beaten bloody, and one of the retainers picked him up and tossed him outside the gate, as one would an unwanted kitten.

Fukutomi's wounds pained him and a strong odor clung to his person; but these things did not bother him so much. What he had to struggle to endure was the bitterness of having been taken in, utterly taken in, by Hidetake. Naturally he hated him, but he was also angry at himself for being gulled. Also, he was ashamed of being so easily misled by the old witch's flattery. He writhed in humiliation at having failed at this, his one great chance. Then, too, there was the fear of going home. What would his wife say? And how disappointed his daughter-in-law would be! And his grandchild, he would be expecting a fine present. No, he didn't feel like going home, and found it impossible to move from the spot. He even felt like ending it all right there; but then the faces of his family floated up before him, and he could not.

He had sat there for a good long time when at last he raised himself shakily, clinging to the cart which had, like himself, been reduced to wreckage. He managed to stand and, dragging the cart along after him, started to walk. People on the street, looking at this sad figure of a man, held their noses and laughed out loud: "My, my, what strange things one sees on the streets!"

Fukutomi's wife was waiting impatiently for his return. Looking at the faces of her daughter-in-law and grandchild, she told them, "Grandpa'll be bringing back a whole cartload of treasures. Yes, we'll be getting beautiful new clothes now; no need for the rags we've been wearing. I'll burn all this trash, so there'll be room for the treasures he's bringing." With the help of her daughter-in-law she set to work, throwing old household articles and ragged clothing into the fire.

But her husband's return was strangely delayed. A bit worried, she sent her grandchild out to look for him, and then continued hurling broken items into the flames. The daughter-in-law looked regretful at the waste, but the woman laughed at her: "You'd think you were born to be poor. We're *rich* now, I tell you!" Just then the child returned to report that he'd seen Grandpa three blocks away, wearing a funny-looking red kimono and pulling his cart so slowly he was hardly moving.

"Ah, he must have gotten a fine crimson robe from the lieutenant general. He couldn't wait till he got home to try it on. And the cart must be just loaded with presents—too heavy for him to pull, really. Well, shall we all go and give him a hand?" And so the three of them set off to meet Fukutomi on the way.

Soon enough they had clear sight of him. He wasn't wearing a fine crimson robe—his clothes were covered with blood. Behind him he wearily dragged the empty cart. Stunned, his wife ran up to him and grabbed him. He just repeated the words "loose bowels" and burst out crying. At those words, coupled with the sight of her husband, the woman understand everything.

"Idiot! Numskull! Botching your biggest chance like that!" she scolded. Even so, having helped her bloodied husband home, she removed his kimono, covered with urine and feces, and was about to cover his nakedness with fresh clothes when she discovered that there were none—she had burned them all. Then she began to massage his legs, naked as he was; the more she rubbed, the stronger the smell that emerged from his body. For the second time, she took him to the well and poured bucketfuls of water over him, but still the smell did not quickly disappear. When at last it did, she put him to bed naked under their thin quilts, called the doctor and had his wounds treated. Her husband, overcome by exhaustion, fell into a dead sleep.

Fukutomi's wounds healed in about a month, but he still had problems with his stomach and bowels. Everything he ate came out as watery diarrhea; he had lost the ability to control his bowels and constantly dirtied himself. Ever since that day he had remained in bed, speaking to no one. It seemed as if he were only waiting for death to come. And, some three months after the incident at the residence, he did die, covered in his own filth. At that point the daughter-in-law decided to leave, taking her child with her. The widow was left alone in the house, still reeking from her husband's illness. As she thought over what had happened, her hatred for Hidetake, who had ruined her husband, grew and grew. Certainly she would have her revenge—she would *kill* him. . . . Thus, the demon of vengeance took hold of her.

The renowned "Master of Farting," however, now seldom appeared on the streets. His usual concerts on Suzaku Avenue grew rare. He performed only at the lieutenant general's, to the delight of the Grand Councilors and Middle

Councilors, and even the Emperor. If the old witch tried to visit his house on Fifth Avenue, she could expect no more than to be turned away at the gate. And so she resigned herself to lying in wait for him on Suzaku Avenue. "He's bound to come back here—it's where all his success began. He'll never forget this place, and he'll come back." Day after day, in the wind and the rain, she crouched on Suzaku Avenue, waiting for Hidetake to show himself.

It was a bright spring day. Drawn, it may be, by the glorious sunny weather, the celebrated Master of Farting came strolling down Suzaku Avenue all by himself, without any attendants. The passersby gazed at him respectfully and told one another how fortunate they were to catch a glimpse of the great Master Takamuku Hidetake in such a place as this. Aware of the whispering voices, Hidetake felt very pleased with himself and moved down the avenue with the calm, assured gait of the great man.

Suddenly something black butted into him from the side of the road. It was the witch, her hair bristling, her eyes drawn up into slits, her mouth a red gash extending to her ears. She sank her teeth into one of Hidetake's breasts. He cried out in pain, for a moment not grasping what was happening to him. He tried frantically to push the black thing away, but it held on with the strength of a lifetime's resentment.

The witch's teeth gnawed at his breast as if to tear it off, like a snapping turtle that would die before letting go of its prey. Hidetake writhed and struggled, but she held on. "You lying little *fart!*" she growled, and kept on biting.

Lazybones Tarō

In the village of Atarashi in the Chikuma region of Shinano province, there lived a man called Lazybones Tarō. It was, of course, just a nickname, but there was no one who called him anything else: he was Lazybones Tarō to one and all. Perhaps he himself had forgotten his real name.

According to the story passed on like a local legend in the village, when he was born he uttered the single syllable "wa," the normal "waugh-waugh" being just too much of an effort. He took only his mother's milk until the age of three; and that only because the breast was brought right up to his mouth. He was never known to cry and demand the breast because he was hungry. The infant Lazybones seemed to feel that it would be better to go to his eternal rest than to do anything so vulgar, and effortful, as crying for food.

When he was three, his mother left his father and perforce also Lazybones. There must have been some compelling reason to make her abandon her own dear child, just turned three, but no one in the village knew what it might

be since the whole family lived as outsiders in Atarashi. His parents had drifted into the village shortly before his birth. The father was originally from the capital; but what he had done there, and why he had come to live in distant Shinano, was a mystery to the villagers. When asked about it, the father would say only that it didn't matter, or that it was so long ago he no longer remembered.

Thus Tarō's family lived a shadowy sort of existence in Atarashi, never mingling with the residents, their only link being O-roku, a neighbor woman who acted as maid-servant. When he came to the village, the father had brought with him some one hundred books and an old-fashioned *biwa* lute, and he spent his days reading and playing the lute. As the years passed, however, he read and played music less and less, spending most of his time staring vacantly into space.

When his mother left the household, she hugged Tarō tight and told him, "I have to leave your father's house today. That means we must say goodbye forever." Having to part from her son like this, she must have been overcome with memories, for large tears began to roll down her cheeks. She tried to say something more but could not speak for crying. For two hours she wept until no more tears would come. Then she said in a strained voice, "Tarō, you can't go on being so lazy. Starting tomorrow, look on O-roku as your mama, and eat everything she gives you."

She hoped her Tarō would stop being so lazy, at least when it came to eating. Little Tarō opened his eyes wide in wonder and looked doubtfully at his weeping mother, but gave only a little nod in response. Even that seemed to set her mind at ease, though, and saying, "You understand, Tarō? Well, Mama has to go now. Goodbye," she hurried off without a backward glance.

And so Tarō was deprived of his mother; but from the

very next day he began to treat O-roku as his mama, as he'd been told to do. He showed no signs of longing for his real mother and ate everything O-roku gave him. The boy had superb powers of forgetfulness, and seemed soon to forget not only his mother but even the fact that he had ever had one.

From then on time passed uneventfully for Tarō until, at the age of eighteen, he experienced another parting. His father had taken to his bed for two or three days with what seemed to be a minor illness when suddenly he left this world on his journey to the next. Tarō consulted with O-roku and arranged for the usual ceremonies—the funeral, and the memorial services on the seventh, the twenty-seventh, and finally the forty-ninth day. Then he immediately sold off the house and household furnishings and built a simple little hut on a small plot facing the road. He explained his plans to O-roku: "I want to lead a totally lazy life from now on. By 'a lazy life,' I mean lying around doing nothing, day and night. There's a saying, 'The greatest pleasure in this life is a good snooze,' and I plan to enjoy my earthly paradise right here in this little hut. But there is one problem, one obstacle to my life of laziness, and that's the fact that a man has to *eat*. Just think how simple it would be if he didn't! Why, men would easily have become like gods. By the way, O-roku, I have some money left over from selling the old house and furniture, and after paying for this hut. This is all the money I have in the world now. I figure it'll pay for my food for about the next five years. And as far as food goes, I won't cause you any trouble, I promise: three rice balls and a pot of tea each morning is all I'll be needing."

O-roku didn't quite know how to respond to Tarō's suggestion so she consulted her son Shichisuke, who said, "That'll mean a big profit for us. If that's all he wants, the money would easily last ten years—maybe twenty, if you cut corners. Anyway, we're sure to make a profit. You're a lucky woman, Mother, to have such a fool for a master. You'd better say yes."

O-roku was worried about what Tarō would do when the five years were up, but he responded, "We'll worry about that when the time comes. Anyway, I want to hibernate for the next five years." With this reply, and encouraged by Shichisuke, O-roku decided to go along with the plan. Shichisuke took care to let the people of the neighborhood think that his mother had received only a fifth of the money she actually had, so everyone praised her for being such a kind-hearted person and taking such good care of her former master's son.

Thus Tarō had succeeded in reducing the energy he expended in the act of eating to a minimum, but there remained one other bothersome aspect of human life to be dealt with: excretion. A man has to go to the bathroom several times a day to take care of this need. Unless he could find a way to minimize the energy used in going to the bathroom, his lazy way of life would remain a dream. So Tarō devised a clever plan and put it into effect. He had a long narrow hole dug in the earth below his sleeping-mat, just where his buttocks rested when he lay down. Then he cut a round hole in the corresponding section of the mat. Now he could urinate while lying face down and defecate face up. Thus he was able to cut to an absolute minimum the energy involved in excretion. There was at first a problem with the smell from below; but he devised a solution to that by making a lid for the hole in the earth and a drawstring for the one in the sleeping mat, so once his business was done, everything could be put back to normal.

Despite these elaborate measures, Tarō's room was not very pleasant. He couldn't seem to get those three daily rice-balls into his mouth without scattering grains of rice here and there; sometimes, too, he accidentally stepped on a rice-ball, so there were clots of mashed rice all over the floor. Then too, he often forgot to close the lid after going to the toilet, and sometimes neglected to wipe himself; so the room was spattered with excrement, liquid and solid, and gave off a truly horrendous stench. Innumerable flies alighted on the bits of rice and feces, and great clusters of them covered Tarō's rice-balls. He was, in effect, eating their leftovers day after day. Tarō was completely unconcerned, however, and happily munched away at his rice-balls, occasionally getting a fly or two along with them. "Sorry, sorry, " he'd say to the flies, "I almost ate you up! By the way, how was the rice today? Good?"

Tarō's room was a world where feces and rice, urine and tea were jumbled together. The smell was worse than a pigsty, and no one would go near the place apart from O-roku. That was fine with Tarō—he could enjoy his lazy life unhindered.

And what precisely did he do all day, in this lazy life of his? Certainly he read a little, for he had kept five books out of the hundred owned by his father and placed them by the bed. Alas, however, even those five books became covered with rice-grains and excrement and lay scattered in disorder beside his pillow. Later on, Tarō would explain that in the course of this lazy way of life he was cultivating his imaginative powers. Now imagination is a convenient thing: in actuality, Tarō dwelt in a filthy hut, but in imagination he could live in the most splendid of houses. Tarō could freely create in his mind a grand mansion and then see himself as its noble inhabitant.

Sometimes, of course, even he tired of these imaginings; yet he was never bored by his life because he could always enjoy the pleasure of conversation with his guests—those guests being the flies. At first he had tried to drive them off, but no matter what he did, they were impossible to get rid of. And so he decided it would be best to make friends with them. Observed with a sympathetic eye, the flies proved to have their own individual traits and personal characteristics. For example, when O-roku brought the rice-balls, some of the flies immediately alighted on them, while others would avoid them and make for the grains of rice sticking to Tarō's lips and chin. Still others would ignore the rice completely and seek out excrement. After the most painstaking observation, Tarō succeeded in distinguishing one fly from another and became aware of these individual differences. To him, this was a great discovery, and he spent the next half year or so in the most intense study of fly society. As he came to understand the ecology of their society, he was able to form friendships with the flies and engage them in conversation.

"Well, Gurukichi, what good wind has blown you in my direction today? It's been a long time, you know. I guess you don't like my rice-balls anymore: I bet you're buzzing around looking for something more to your taste. What's that? You say you had a good feast on some bear's liver the day before yesterday? And yesterday you had a *real* delicacy, dragon's brains? And today you drank some cat-wine brought all the way from Southern Barbary? My rice-balls can't compete in terms of flavor, you say? Yes, well, that's fine. It's fine with me, Gurukichi, but you're putting yourself in real danger. I'm happy to have you fellows come over for some rice-balls; but, you know, gourmets tend to be stingy, and cruel too. You wouldn't think they'd lose much by letting a few flies have a nibble at their food; but I think you'll find they'll get hopping mad and be after you with a fly-swatter. One swat with one of those and you'll be flat as a pancake! Ohh, you think you're too smart to let some human half-wit get you with a fly-swatter? Don't be too sure of yourself, Gurukichi.

It's dangerous, I tell you, very dangerous. You'll end up swatted one of these days. It'd be better for you to come and have rice-balls with me. It may not be very delicious, but it's safe. And anyway, it's rather vulgar to spend your time flying about looking for better and better things to eat. You should avoid such base behavior."

Gurukichi listened to these admonitions with a bored expression, as if to say "Yes, yes, I know all that." He never reappeared at Tarō's hut, though, and it was said that he had been swatted to death in the kitchen of a rich landowner a block or so away.

"Nauko, you're the best-looking fly I've ever seen. You're always being followed by a swarm of boy-flies. You lead them around as you buzz about, lost in wonder at your own beauty. 'I'm the most beautiful creature on earth,' you seem to be saying to yourself. But be careful! It's not only boy-flies, under the spell of sex, who are watching you. There are bees and dragonflies that would love to eat you up. And spiders are very fond of flies, too. I heard some of them talking just the other day: 'That Nauko looks *real* good. Let's get her,' they were saying. So don't get too infatuated with your own looks. They're not that special, to begin with. A butterfly would think herself far more beautiful than you. And a bird would be sure she was much more beautiful than any butterfly. And the same for humans. Now, I think even the handsomest human is uglier than a bird or butterfly—or a fly, for that matter; but there *are* human beings (particularly among the females) who believe themselves to be the most beautiful creatures on earth. Anyway, it's dangerous to fall in love with your own beauty!"

Nauko laughed as she listened to what Tarō had to say, but she too never appeared again. According to her boyfriend, who was always hanging around her, she was buzzing about engrossed in herself one day when suddenly a bird flew by and gobbled her up.

Tarō also spoke with Dobuhei, whose favorite spot was the area around his mouth, with the grains of rice sticking there. "You always used to like being around waste-matter, didn't you, Dobuhei? You lived in an outhouse for years: your body smells of it. So why did you decide to move, and pick the area around my mouth?" Tarō asked this question many times, but Dobuhei wouldn't answer, until finally one day he gave this unwilling reply: "I like dirty places, and I find the smell of night-soil wonderfully fragrant. I couldn't live a single day without it. But, you know, an outhouse is a dangerous place. You never know when someone's going to take a crap—you could be crushed! Your mouth is a much safer place. And it has much the same smell, too. The smell of crap and sweat and dirt and garbage, all combined together—wonderful! And it's all so nourishing: spit and snot and sweat mixed in with the rice stuck here—what could be more delicious? So I decided, from now on forget about outhouses, I'm staying near Tarō's mouth forever."

"You're quite a guy, Dobuhei. It's like we're brothers!" said Tarō, and from then on he made sure to leave plenty of rice sticking to his lips and chin so his friend would feel right at home.

This was the reality of Tarō's lazy life over a period of five years. Of the twenty-four hours in a day, he slept for twelve and lazed about for another six, mostly fantasizing or observing and chatting with his friends the flies. Of course he also read a little once in a while, just for fun.

The agreed-upon five year period was coming to an end, and O-roku was concerned about what Tarō would do from then on. One day she said timidly, "Master Tarō, the five years we agreed on are up this month. I'm not saying the money you gave me for food for the five years wasn't enough. But prices have risen since then, so the cost of food has been high too. And anyway, we had an agreement. So after this month, I won't be able to provide you with three rice-balls and a pot of tea everyday, like before. . . . Still, you *are* the son of my dear late master, so if you want, I'd be willing to keep on providing the rice-balls and tea—not forever, you understand, but for a while."

Tarō, however, turned down this offer. He thanked O-roku warmly for her devotion over the past five years but said that they'd had an agreement, and from now on there was no need for her to make three daily rice-balls for him.

"Well then, what will you do for food?" she asked.

"Could you please send a notice 'round to the neighbors and ask them to bring me any leftover rice they might have? I'm not trying to force them, of course. If there's rice, I'll eat it, and if there's not, I'll go hungry. If there's no rice for a long time, and I end up dying of starvation, that'll be fine with me too." O-roku was surprised, but she did as Tarō said and asked the neighbors to let her know if there was any leftover rice, so she could take it to him. She was feeling a bit guilty so she made a point of going from house to house each evening to collect the rice, which she then delivered to Tarō. Occasionally too she would make rice-balls for him as before, saying they were someone else's leftovers.

Still, Tarō was not receiving rice as regularly as he had been before. Whenever O-roku took her own rice to him, pretending it was leftovers, her son Shichisuke gave her a dirty look. It sometimes happened, then, that Tarō went without food for several days; even so, he never complained. One day O-roku delivered five special festive rice-cakes to him. "I got something nice today so I brought some along for you!" she said happily. They were large, flat, plate-shaped cakes eaten on the third day after a wedding. One of her relatives had got married and O-roku had been given ten, of which she brought five for Tarō, hiding the fact from her son. Tarō had not eaten anything for four or five days, so he was famished and polished off four of the cakes immediately. Actually, he wanted to eat the last one as well, but he didn't know when he might eat again if he did. So he kept it and played with it, rolling it around on his chest, licking it, rubbing some of the oil from beside his nostrils on it, and balancing it on the top of his head. As he was amusing himself in this fashion, the rice-cake slipped away from him and rolled over the floor, out of the hut, and on to the side of the road. It would have been too much trouble to go and get it. Someone would come along and retrieve it for him, surely. So Tarō waited. But humans aren't the only ones who are fond of rice-cakes. Dogs came, and crows, eyeing the cake by the roadside. Lazybones Tarō kept them off with a pole from inside the hut and waited for a passerby.

On the third day, the local steward, Atarashi Zaemon Nobuyori, passed by on horseback on his way home from a hawking expedition, accompanied by fifty or sixty mounted warriors. As he passed along the road in front of Tarō's hut, the steward heard a strange, harsh-sounding voice calling after him: "Master Steward, Master Steward, Lazybones Master Steward!" Surprised to be so addressed, the steward drew up his horse and approached the hut. A strong odor assailed his nostrils. He threw the door open and walked in. What a terrible sight! A veritable pigsty. It was a wonder to the steward that any human being could live in a place like this. Yet there was Tarō sprawled on the floor, his head raised like a snake about to strike, gazing fixedly at him.

"Are you the famous Lazybones Tarō?" asked the steward.

"That's right—the one and only, the genuine article!"

"I see. Now then, you called me 'Lazybones Steward' just now, didn't you. Why do you call me lazy?"

"Because you *are* lazy. The rice-cake I dropped three days ago is sitting right there by the road, and you couldn't be bothered to pick it up! I'm amazed anybody so lazy can carry out the important duties of a steward."

The steward glanced out and saw that, indeed, a large round rice-cake was sitting by the side of the road. Stunned, he stared at Tarō for a moment and then said, "I see. You really *are* the laziest man in Japan. Tell me, though, how do you get your food?"

"If people give me food, I eat; and if they don't, I don't. Sometimes I go for three or four days without a meal, but even so, I can't give up this lazy life of mine. There's nothing like it. You should give it a try yourself, sir! I'll gladly teach you the rudiments."

"You want me to lead a lazy life? No, no, that won't do. It's you who should give up the lazy life! How about it: if I give you some land, will you become a rice-farmer?"

But this kind offer on the steward's part was flatly rejected: "Absolutely not! I'd rather die than tie myself to some little plot of land."

The steward tried another tack: "Well then, I'll stake you in a business. Why not try your hand at trade?"

"A country man like me wouldn't be good enough at duping people for that."

He's quite a character, thought the steward, and decided to demonstrate his goodheartedness by sponsoring Tarō for a further three years of lazy living. Thus, he ordered the people of Atarashi to provide him with food for the next three years. A troublesome whim of the steward's, from their point of view, but if it were only a matter of having O-roku carry on with the three rice-balls and pot of tea each day, it would be a simple enough demand to satisfy. And so Lazybones Tarō's lazy life was extended for another three years.

The three years' sponsorship was nearing its end when another, more troublesome demand was made of the people of the village. Atarashi was in fact a manor owned by a certain Middle Councilor living in the capital, Kyoto, and managed by the steward assigned for that purpose by the military government in Kamakura. The Middle Councilor had sent an order that someone from the village be despatched at once to the capital for a period of obligatory service, as was the custom in those days. It would involve three months' service, with almost no wages. Naturally, no one in the village was eager to go, yet the order had to be obeyed. The villagers held an assembly to discuss whom to send, but no one would agree to go: everyone, it seemed, had an ill parent at home, or, if they had no parents, had been expressly forbidden at their father's deathbed ever to set foot in the capital. The discussions went on for days without any solution in sight. Suddenly, though, a village elder had a brilliant idea: send Lazybones! He was a burden to the village anyway, so by sending him off to do service, they would be killing two birds with one stone.

The elder, in a state of great excitement, presented his idea to the group, but there were two doubtful points. First, even supposing Tarō agreed to go to the capital, would the people at the Middle Councilor's residence find him of any use at all? Would there not come a complaint against the villagers for sending such a good-for-nothing? Some people had quite strong negative views on this matter; but it was suggested that, if need be, the village could always say that Tarō had been a model worker while in Atarashi, and something must have gone wrong with him after he went to the capital. Someone suggested that, on the other hand, Tarō might in fact change for the better once he got to the capital. By dint of such ingenious arguments, the doubters were silenced, and it was decided by consensus to send Tarō.

The bigger problem was whether he would agree to be sent. If he refused to go, the "great" plan would indeed "grate" on everyone's ears, wouldn't it? Even so, the prevailing view was that they should "make the attempt," "there could be no harm in trying," "what did they have to lose?" and so on. Chōemon, the elder whose idea it was, and Hambei were appointed to go and convince him.

It was the first time either of them had ever visited Tarō's hut, and when they entered, what filth, what a stench! They'd heard gossip, of course, but the reality of the dirt and smells exceeded all expectation. Chōemon held his nose as he began: "Good day to you, Tarō. The three years ordered by the steward are almost up now, and we were all wondering if, you know, you might not like to go off to the capital. There's a grand palace there where the Emperor himself lives! How about going to live at the Middle Councilor's place in the Emperor's capital? Ahh, it's a fine mansion, and there's lots of pretty girls living there too. It'd be like a sightseeing trip for you. You could stay, oh, about three months and do a little work now and then for the Middle Councilor. What's that you say? A man like yourself, used to a lazy life for such a long time, is unable to work? Not at all, Tarō! You've given your body a good long rest these past years, and now you're brimming with energy! And, you know, it's not *healthy* to lie about *too* much. Work is the thing for health! And though I say 'work,' what you'd be doing in the capital is much easier than the farm work that goes on here in the village. So how about it, Tarō, won't you go?"

Now Chōemon and Hambei fully expected an initial refusal, so they were surprised to hear Tarō's reply: "I'll go, of course I'll go. I'll be glad to go to the capital."

While leading his lazy life, Tarō had fantasized daily about living in a grand mansion and becoming a Middle Councilor, or a Grand Councilor, or even Emperor. What could be better, therefore, than to go to the capital? From that very day, he gave up his life of idleness and said goodbye to his longtime companions in solitude, the flies. Then, bidding farewell to the villagers, he set out on his journey. Relieved at getting rid of this burden to the village and at having carried out the Middle Councilor's command, the people of Atarashi sent Tarō off loaded with gifts. There was considerable unease, however, as to whether he would actually do the work required by his obligatory service.

Having despatched Tarō to the capital, they lived in fear of receiving any day now a reprimand from Kyoto. When a messenger did come, however, he brought unexpected news: Tarō was a very hard worker, and the Middle Councilor was highly pleased. True, he had the strange habit of going round to look at the mansions of the Grand Councilors and Ministers and even the palace of the Emperor, on his day off; but that did not really matter, and the Middle Councilor was warm in his praise for Tarō's devoted service.

As if this news were not surprise enough for the villagers of Atarashi, some four months later there came word of developments a hundred times more startling. Having finished his period of service, Tarō remained in the capital, going to Kiyomizu Temple every day to look among the worshippers for a suitable bride. The woman he found at last was the favorite attendant of the wife of a Grand Councilor. They got to know each other through an exchange of poems; and, though at first she was not interested in him, she was gradually won over by his evident cultivation as well as gentleness. In the end, she became his bride.

However, this second piece of news seemed rather ordinary by comparison with the third, which was to come. This last was truly earth-shaking: heaven and earth could have crumbled to pieces without producing more amazement among the people of Atarashi. The news was that Tarō was the son of the Prince of Uji, himself the son of a previous Emperor. The Prince of Uji had been banished to Shinano on false charges and had died there. Tarō was, in fact, the son of this prince and a local woman. It had by now become clear to everyone that the charges against the prince had been groundless. Thus, when the Court learned that Tarō was actually his surviving heir, he was granted the fifth court rank and appointed governor of Shinano, the place of his father's undeserved exile. He was expected to return and take up his duties there very soon.

This news was truly gut-wrenching to the people of Atarashi. If the story had begun and ended in the capital, amazement would have been their only response; but if Lazybones Tarō was to come to Shinano as governor, it would have a great effect on their own destinies. Atarashi was, after all, Tarō's hometown. One normally feels affection for one's hometown, so the new governor would almost certainly do well by the people of Atarashi. That was one viewpoint. But there were persons who very much doubted whether Tarō would feel grateful toward the village, given its treatment of him and his family over the years. The villagers had never dreamed that the man who, some thirty years before, had appeared from nowhere to lead a shadowy existence in their midst had been in reality an august personage of imperial rank. True, they need not accuse themselves of grossly abusing the family of strangers, but neither had they gone out of their way to be kind. And as for Tarō (the son of an Imperial Prince!) with his unaccountable lazy ways, the villagers had always viewed him with contempt as an eccentric, and mocked him as a fool. If they had sent him to the capital, it was to be rid of a tiresome nuisance. Why should Tarō feel goodwill toward people who had treated him like that? No doubt he would pay them back with some punishment as soon as he took up his new post. When one of their number expressed this opinion, the fear of impending punishment spread throughout Atarashi, and the people trembled.

There was nothing left for it but to seek the help of O-roku, the only person in Atarashi who had shown kindness to Tarō. Suddenly the old woman became a person of importance, kowtowed to by all the villagers, who asked that she go to Government House and beg the new governor's pardon on behalf of Atarashi, if he imposed some harsh exaction on the village. O-roku herself, however, was secretly afraid that Tarō might have become aware of her trickery regarding the costs of his food; like the other villagers, she feared Tarō's return to Shinano as governor.

Soon afterwards the new governor assumed his post in Shinano, but no message came from him to Atarashi until a half year had passed. His letter stated that Atarashi was his hometown, and that he was grateful especially to O-roku for her kindness. Chōemon and the other elders too had been good enough to send him to the capital, which had led to his present good fortune. He wished to thank O-roku, Chōemon, and the others in person, and asked them to present themselves at the governor's mansion.

Reading the letter, the inhabitants of Atarashi heaved a collective sigh of relief, and Chōemon and the other elders, together with O-roku, went off to Government House. When they arrived, they were amazed at the beauty of the governor's residence. It was not that it was sumptuous or obviously costly. It had, rather, an elegant refinement combined throughout with a highly functional design: it was this that was so impressive. And the entire edifice had apparently been designed by the governor (that is to say, by Lazybones Tarō), who had given detailed instructions to the builders. It was hard for the villagers of Atarashi to believe that their Lazybones had been responsible for such an impressive structure.

As they stood there gaping, the governor appeared. He certainly resembled Lazybones; but they simply could not connect the dignified person of the governor, his hair carefully arranged, with the old Tarō, living in a smelly hut, with hair disheveled, body grimy, and rice sticking to his mouth. They were stunned into silence, and the governor too said nothing. The silence continued for a while until the governor broke it by saying, "Welcome, people of Atarashi. I remember you all fondly."

They didn't know quite what to say to this; but, overwhelmed by the series of shocks, one of them found himself asking a rather rude question: "Are y-y-you really Master Lazybones? We never dreamed Lazybones would become His Excellency the Governor . . ."

"A man is an animal that's constantly changing," the governor replied with a smile. "The 'me' of yesterday is not the same as the 'me' of today. Therefore, the Lazybones Tarō of ten years ago is not the same as the man who stands before you now. On the other hand, I do have some memory of him, deep inside me, so perhaps I *am* the same person after all."

The villagers didn't really understand what this reply might mean, and they asked him another unseemly question: "We're happy to have the chance to see your official residence, Your Excellency. It's wonderful—there's nothing else like it here in the provinces. And we hear that it was Your Excellency himself, the former Master Lazybones, who designed it and oversaw its building. It's incredible to us who knew Master Lazybones that he could ever have built anything as wonderful as this. We've also heard rumors that Master Lazybones wooed his present wife, the attendant at the Grand Councilor's residence, by writing poems to her.

This too doesn't seem at all like the man we knew. Did you *really* build this mansion and *really* write those poems?"

Once again Master Lazybones smiled and responded to their rude inquiry:

"Among the books my father left me, there was the plan for a mansion—probably his old residence in the capital, I suppose. And there were more plans of other mansions as well. I looked at them everyday and imagined the kind of house I'd like to live in, building it and tearing it down and rebuilding it in my mind. Then when I went to Kyoto, I walked around looking at mansions belonging to various people. So when I was appointed governor and came back to Shinano, I knew how to realize my dream of so many years—though I didn't have the funds to do more than what you see.

"Among my father's books, there was also a copy of *Poems, Ancient and Modern*. If you live an idle life for eight years, it's not hard to memorize the poems in that collection. I varied them slightly when I exchanged poems with the lady who became my wife. That gave rise to all sorts of amusing gossip!"

He laughed heartily. The villagers understood what he meant this time, but it was hard for them to imagine Tarō gazing at house-plans and perusing the classical poetry collection in the midst of that lazy life.

Finally the villagers asked the governor what concerned them most: what did he think of them and their village?

"The people of Atarashi were kind to my family; and, in particular, they allowed me to spend eight long years leading the idle life of my choice. I'm grateful for that. O-roku, especially, brought food to me every day; and Chōemon and the others sent me to Kyoto. I'm going to give all of you presents as a sign of my gratitude. " And, distributing various gifts, he sent the villagers away. They returned home rejoicing that Lazybones Tarō had not taken revenge for past grievances, but rather had given them gifts. Still, in all his time in Shinano, the benevolent governor never once went to visit the village of Atarashi, his old hometown.

Lastly, as to the way the governor worked: it was his habit to go to his office daily and take charge of affairs; yet he managed to spend most of his time there reading books and gazing off into space. Occasionally a subordinate would come to ask for his judgment on some matter. "Uh-huh," the governor would say, nodding his head. "That'll be fine. Do as you think best." His residence was of course incomparably larger than Lazybones Tarō's hut; and, since he had a wife, and plenty of maid-servants and retainers, he was never grubby and never had grains of rice sticking to his mouth. But apart from that, his way of life was almost the same as it had been in his days of idleness.

This new governor, who at first sight must have seemed an incompetent, did something which stunned his subordinates in the first year after his arrival: he announced a new personnel policy. He had the splendid idea of enforcing rewards and punishments fairly at every level of government service, including the lowest. Observing the new policy, the provincial officials all knew in their hearts that there was something mysterious and inscrutable about this governor, who still had a good deal of "Lazybones Tarō" about him. Thus, his orders were carried out, and the province of Shinano was well governed. About three times a year, the "Lazybones Governor" would shake his head as he listened to reports from his staff. That meant a clear "no" to what was being proposed; and his subordinates would realize eventually that by doing this he had nipped some troublesome problem in the bud.

He had served as governor for ten years, and then one day his sleeping-mat was found empty. His wife and his retainers scoured the province, its mountains and rivers, but no trace of him was ever found. People began to wonder if this governor, whose early life, sudden rise, and final disappearance were all so strange, might not be a god or spirit. In the end, the ex-governor, Master Lazybones Tarō, came to be worshipped as a god. In his hometown of Atarashi, a shrine was erected to the "Great Luminous Deity Lazybones," and people came to worship there, as they do to this very day.

Lotus

Kumagai Jirō Naozane, after encountering the great saint Hōnen and hearing the doctrine of the Sole Practice of the Nembutsu, immediately shaved his head and took the religious name Rensei-bō ("Lotus-Born"). He did this out of an earnest wish to be reborn on the calyx of a lotus flower in the Pure Land of Perfect Bliss.

Naozane remained for a time in the capital, serving Honen. He may have become a monk, but he was still a fierce warrior from the Eastlands and well fitted to act as the holy man's bodyguard. Hōnen's teachings represented a total revolution in the interpretation of the *nembutsu* and a fundamental denial of the Buddhist doctrines that had prevailed up to that time. For that reason, he was hated by many in the capital, and above all by the monks of the Tendai Sect on Mount Hiei. Hōnen's person was always in danger, and his disciples had been looking for a powerful warrior to defend him; but they could hardly hire a professional in armor and helmet as the holy man's bodyguard.

Thus, Naozane's entry into the monastic community seemed heaven-sent.

And so Rensei-bō served as bodyguard for a time. One day, however, he suddenly said to his teacher, "I would like to return to the East and spread your teachings there." This request surprised the other disciples. He spoke of spreading the teachings, but Rensei-bō was still very much the warrior, a man of violent passions. Who knew what he might do? The disciples had misgivings. But Hōnen gathered the community together and addressed them: "There are many enemies of the *nembutsu* in the East. It will take a man like Rensei-bō, with his intense, pure-hearted faith, to spread the teachings there."

It is said that when Rensei-bō heard tell of this, he said: "Hōnen is the only one who truly understands me. I'm willing to give my life for my teacher!"

Rensei-bō bade farewell to Hōnen and the disciples and set off for the East in high spirits, but he presented a very odd appearance as he traveled. He had already made a name for himself as a master archer and horseman, yet before reaching his destination, he fell from his horse any number of times. And no wonder: the horse's head was set toward the East, but he had reversed the saddle, putting it back to front, so he rode facing backwards. Asked why, he answered, "The West is the direction where Lord Amida resides. It would be rude to sit with my backside to that direction."

It had been a long time since he'd returned to his native Musashi. Burned into the minds of the people of that province was the image of Kumagai Jirō Naozane, the daredevil of the battle of Ichinotani. It was said that Naozane had now entered religion and become a disciple of Hōnen, but it was impossible for the people of Musashi to conceive of this wild warrior tonsured. That was why crowds of people came day after day to his lodgings, hoping for a glimpse of the new Rensei-bō. He welcomed them warmly and explained just how he had become a *nembutsu* devotee.

"Over the years I've built up a lot of bad karma for myself, and I've suffered as a result. But now that I'm a disciple of Hōnen, I've found happiness," he began in a gentle voice. Then all of a sudden, his face turned red and he began to shout: "Shame on you all! You're still attached to this world of dust and keep on piling up bad karma. Shame on you! Hurry up and enter the Way of Sole Practice! Concentrate on rebirth in paradise!"

His audience, watching the monk Rensei-bō haranguing them and recalling the former fierce warrior Kumagai Jirō Naozane, felt a touch of nostalgia, and a touch of the burlesque. Yet there were many, too, who were moved by the intensity of his faith, and large numbers of them became *nembutsu* devotees as a result.

Viewed from outside, Naozane's entry into the religious life seemed surprising, but it was by no means a sudden decision on his part. He had made a name for himself as a valiant fighter in the Genji-Heike wars and then returned to his native place, but deep in his heart he was sick of being a warrior. Of course he enjoyed the thrill of battle. He loved the tense excitement: the two camps pitched over against each other; the single horseman slipping from his own camp, riding out in front of the enemy and announcing in a loud voice: "It is I, Kumagai Jirō Naozane, dweller in the land of Musashi!" He truly loved this instant when he took the lead in beginning the battle. Then, ignoring the hail of arrows released by the enemy archers, he would plunge into the enemy camp, cutting down the warriors who, one after another, came at him with slashing swords. Could anything in the world be as thrilling? Even now Naozane's heart would beat faster at the memory of those moments on the battlefield.

It was at the battle of Satake that he first experienced the excitement of leading the initial charge. He rode far ahead of everyone else and killed many of the enemy. There were some who later criticized his impetuous act as contrary to military regulations, but it was hard to deny that his courage in pressing alone into the enemy camp greatly raised the fighting-spirit of his own side and led them to an overwhelming victory. This battle of Satake made military men aware of Naozane's existence, but it was the battle of Ichinotani above all that made him famous throughout the land.

In this latter battle, he took the head of Atsumori, scion of the Heike clan. When he did so, he recalled for a moment Kojirō, his own son of the same age; but it was only a moment's hesitation. The account passed down to later ages of Naozane's motive for becoming a monk—his striking down Atsumori, the Heike noble of seventeen, and his "weeping, weeping as he struck"; his consequent sense of the transience of life, leading to his taking the tonsure—all of this was a lie, made up by monks who made their living telling stories. In reality, Naozane never forgot his joy at taking the head of Atsumori, son of the Heike.

Why, then, did this man so fond of battle come to dislike the life of the soldier? It is not enough for a soldier simply to fight day after day. After the battle comes the duty to report to his superiors, which can result in a heightened reputation for valor and other rewards. To Naozane, however, it was a great nuisance. This was true after the battle of Ichinotani as well. Kajiwara Heizō Kagetoki inquired of him: "How many heads did you, in fact, take? I've heard about Atsumori, but I want a report on how many heads you took in all."

"It must have been twenty or thirty; I don't remember anything beyond that."

"That's no good! You have to tell me exactly how many—and provide proof as well," said Kagetoki sharply.

The number of men killed is very important in warfare. But to Naozane, it was a matter of kill or be killed: he fought desperately with all his strength against the enemies who presented themselves one after another. For him, to fight was ecstasy, and in ecstasy one forgets to remember. In that respect, a battle is like sex. Sex leaves only the memory of ecstasy—one has no sense of having done this or that. In just the same way, if one remembered each and every action in battle, it was a sign that one had not forgotten oneself, had not fought with every ounce of one's being—that was Naozane's view. Fighters, after bringing down an enemy, always cut off a hank of hair or ripped off some ornament the dead man was wearing, as proof of the kill; but to Naozane that seemed unbefitting a warrior. Thus, he always left the battlefield empty-handed.

Kagetoki demanded again, "'Twenty or thirty' won't do. Give me a definite number."

"I don't remember the number," said Naozane.

"You're causing me a lot of trouble. What shall I say to Lord Yoritomo? I can't tell him you say twenty or maybe thirty, but offer no proof!"

This made Naozane very angry. "Please tell the Shōgun precisely that. 'Naozane says he took twenty or thirty heads, but he's lying.' Why don't you report it to the Shōgun like that?"

Having said that, he turned on his heel and left. As a result, though both he and almost everyone else believed he had taken the greatest number of heads in the battle, he was listed in third place. Of course, he was furious at this result.

Still, the days when he could go out and do battle were not so bad. It was when the battles were ended and everyday life returned that a man like Naozane, who lived only for the excitement of warfare, was at a loss to know what to do with himself. Other men used the reputations they had gained on the battlefield to enrich and advance themselves, insatiably. For when peace came, the military government in Kamakura had more use for the talents of politicians skilled in administration and versed in scholarship and the law—men like Ōe Hiromoto, who wore the "long sleeves" of the civil official. Warriors who formerly galloped their horses proudly over the battlefield now tried to win Ōe Hiromoto's favor and spent their energies on lawsuits and the quest for promotion. Naozane found the lot of them unbearably offensive.

One day he received a summons from the military government concerning a lawsuit, the kind of thing he hated most. His uncle Kuge Naomitsu had appealed to the military authorities in support of a claim to a portion of the lands in the Kumagai area, a claim which seemed utterly ridiculous to Naozane. The Kumagai lands had been in the family for generations, handed down from his ancestors to his father and from his father to himself. Everyone knew that. So why would his maternal uncle Kuge Naomitsu insist they were his? He couldn't begin to understand.

It was true that he had left the lands in his uncle's care when he went off to fight in the Genji-Heike wars. All the men of the clan, young and old, were leaving the Eastlands to take part in the wars; but that meant leaving his wife and child behind. So Naozane had been casting about for someone to take care of his family and lands during his absence. Calling to mind the pallid face of his uncle Naomitsu, he felt sure *he* would not be eager to participate in the campaign; moreover, being weak and sickly, he would pose no threat to Naozane's wife and child. He decided to invite his uncle over and make his request.

"I would like to join the rest of you and drive out the Heike, but I've been in ill health lately and I can't go just now. I'd planned to rush off to the wars just as soon as I'm better, though. But if you really want me to stay here and guard your family and lands, I would be willing to do so," said Naomitsu.

"Liar," thought Naozane. Of course he was not planning to join the campaign. If someone like him went off to battle, he'd die before he caught sight of the enemy. He'd be nothing but a nuisance in a military camp. Naozane wouldn't dream of taking him along even if he begged him to.

"I understand your desire to join the campaign, Uncle; but I'd be grateful if you'd change your mind and look after things here. I'd like you to move here and take charge of the fief, if that's possible for you."

At these words, a smile spread across his uncle's wan-looking face. "Your humble servant Kuge Naomitsu will be honored to guard your possessions in your absence to the very best of his poor abilities. Set your mind at rest as you go off to the wars."

So Naozane joined the campaign and, after winning much honor, returned to Kumagai. His uncle welcomed him back with a show of great humility, was as submissive to his nephew as a family retainer, and hurried to carry out any orders that were given. And not only that, he even anticipated Naozane's desires in the slightest things, without waiting to be asked.

Truly, his uncle had taken very good care of things while Naozane was away. His wife and child had lived free from care, and the management of the fief had been flawless. As a sign of his gratitude, Naozane gave him a portion of the lands in Chichibu which the government had allotted to him. Naomitsu, however, stayed on in Kumagai and continued to manage the fief. Naozane raised no objections to this: managerial affairs were a nuisance to him, and he was grateful his uncle was willing to handle them for him. Now Naomitsu began to fawn on his nephew and flatter him all the more, but Naozane disliked fawners and flatterers. He firmly believed that no man should lower himself that much to anyone whomsoever. And so he decided to remove his uncle from the household.

"I appreciated your looking after things during my long absence, but I don't like your ways, Uncle. Please leave my house." At this, Naomitsu left Kumagai without a word and moved to the lands in Chichibu which he had received from Naozane earlier.

And now, suddenly, there was this lawsuit. Naomitsu was claiming to have a deed of gift from Naozane's father, Naosada. How could there be such a thing? His father had also disliked Naomitsu; he would never have given him so much as a square yard of the Kumagai lands. Yet the deed of gift was supposed to grant a full half of the lands to Naomitsu.

If his uncle had written evidence in support of his lawsuit, then Naozane should have some of his own for rebuttal—even *he* knew that much. But why should documents be necessary in a case as simple and clear-cut as this, he wondered. Hadn't documents been invented in the first place only after human beings began to tell lies? His uncle's written evidence was a downright forgery, and downright lies should be met with an upright heart! If there was no dishonesty in his own heart, his uncle's deceptions would easily be revealed for what they were. Thus, Naozane took the matter rather lightly, not bothering to devise any countermeasures and going into the conflict unarmed, as it were.

However, since his uncle had appealed to the military government, the suit would be decided by a board of judges whose representative was Ōe Hiromoto, Naozane's *bête noire*. Naozane was unhappy about this, but there was nothing he could do: he had to respond to the government's summons. So he appeared unwillingly before Hiromoto, who first of all demanded that both he and his uncle formally identify themselves. When that formality was over, he showed Naozane the deed of gift and asked him what he thought of it. Naozane had to admit that the handwriting looked like his father's, and the signature also seemed authentic. Finally, it was dated from a period when his father had been ill.

As Naozane tried to recall the events of that time, Hiromoto produced yet another document. This was addressed to Naomitsu's elder brother Naotake and included the following statement: "I am now ill, and my sons are often absent from the Eastlands, off on distant campaigns. They have no time to care for me. You and your brother, however, have been very good to me in my illness. I am most grateful, and I plan to give you my fiefdom, at some convenient time." Here too, the handwriting and signature seemed to be his father's, just as with the deed of gift. For a moment Naozane himself wondered if his father might have written it; but he knew his father would never have given his principal fief to others outside the family, setting aside his own sons to do so. No, he would not have done that, no matter how ill and weakened in body and spirit he might have been. It was a brazen forgery—it had to be!

"Certainly the handwriting and signature look very much like my father's. Or rather, were *made* to look very like them. But they're blatant forgeries—the deed of gift is a forgery, and so is this letter of intent. How dare you fabricate things like this to try to fool the authorities, you black-hearted villain!" He shouted out the last words, glaring fiercely at Naomitsu.

"I represent the Shōgun himself. You are not to shout in my presence. You had better calm yourself and respond to my questions. All right?" Then, after a short pause, Hiromoto resumed. "Why do you judge this letter to be a forgery? Give me your reasons."

"To hell with 'reasons'! In the first place, what father would set his own son aside and give his lands to an outsider? I am the eldest son and heir. 'Heir' means the one who inherits! It's self-evident that I should inherit all of my father's lands. And now this ungrateful villain comes up with some papers and takes me to court! His death would make the world a better place."

"You speak very threateningly," Hiromoto replied. "And 'heir' means the one who inherits, does it? What a learned man you are! But I have no desire to listen to your displays of learning. It is up to you to prove that the two documents presented by Master Naomitsu are indeed forgeries. We need written evidence that your father intended to leave all his land in Kumagai to you—that, or clear evidence proving that these two documents are counterfeit. Without one or the other, I regret to tell you that the judgment will go against you. Now then, may we see your evidence?"

Naozane felt anger boiling inside him as he listened to Hiromoto's slow, leisurely manner of speaking.

"I have the evidence. I have it right here!" he exclaimed, pointing to his belly. "We Eastern warriors do not tell lies, unlike courtiers from the capital. If you doubt my word, I will cut open my belly and show you the honesty of my heart!"

Hiromoto showed some surprise: "No, no, spare me that. I have no desire to see the nasty insides of your stomach. What is needed now is not 'the honesty of your heart,' but proper evidence."

With this, Naozane lost all control: "Never mind. I give all the land to Naomitsu!" Taking out his sword, he cut off his topknot and threw it in Hiromoto's long, horse-like face. He then walked out.

Naozane was sick, sick and tired of everything—of Kamakura, of the Shōgun's government, of warriors and all their ways. He wanted to flee from all three. Where would he flee to? He had no idea. He felt like running to the very ends of the earth.

His horse, however, seemed of itself to go westward, westward toward the capital. The reason was that the image of a certain man was burned into Naozane's heart. The day before the battle of Ichinotani, he saw by chance a monk whose appearance inspired awe. That monk was the holy Shōkaku, a disciple of Hōnen who was held in even higher reverence than his master by the aristocrats of the capital.

It was late by the time he reached Kyoto, but, ignoring the hour, Kumagai Naozane knocked at Shōkaku's door. The monk got up, wondering what it could be, and found standing at his gate an unkempt, hairy-faced fellow of rather fearful aspect. For a moment the holy man was frightened, but the other begged, "Save me, please. Help me. My name is Kumagai Jirō Naozane, and I have given up being a warrior to come here. They say you guide people to a good place called Amida's Pure Land—please, reverend sir, take me there!"

Of course Shōkaku had heard of Kumagai Jirō Naozane, the famous warrior. But why had he decided to quit his present life? The monk was still a bit uneasy, but he said to his visitor: "You have learned to despise the world, and that is a good thing. The High Priest Eshin, who laid the foundations of the Pure Land School here in Japan, said that the first step toward developing faith in the Pure Land is to despise this present, ugly world and separate oneself from it. But it is a very difficult matter to lead a brave warrior like yourself to the Pure Land of Perfect Bliss. It is beyond my abilities. I think the only one who could guide you there is my teacher, Master Hōnen. You should go and visit him tomorrow."

So the next day Naozane went to see Hōnen at his hermitage in Yoshimizu. When he arrived, the holy man had already begun his sermon. A great crowd of people were there, listening to Hōnen's preaching. Some were clearly aristocrats and others warriors, but most were commoners. There were evil-looking fellows who might well have been professional killers; voluptuous women who seemed to have given themselves more to the ways of love than to the Way of the Buddha; and dubious youths who looked too ignorant to understand much of what was being preached to them. Yet, strange to say, all of them were listening to Hōnen's sermon joyfully and attentively: "Now I ask you, my friends—which is easier, to travel by sea or by land? Of course, it makes quite a difference whether you go through the mountains or the plains, if by land, and whether the sea is calm or stormy. But taken all in all, wouldn't we agree that it is easier and faster to go by sea? By the way, where did you people come from? From Awa, in Shikoku? Then you came by sea, and I bet you had a pleasant voyage. A boat trip on a calm sea can be very pleasant! The holy T'an-luan of China said that the Pure Land teachings are like a sea-voyage, fast and easy. The Way of the Sages, the other great Buddhist path, is much harder. It's hard to learn, and hard to put into practice. It's like going by land over steep mountain roads. Why would anyone cast aside the fast, easy, fruitful teachings of the Pure Land in favor of the slow, difficult, and less effectual Way of the Sages?

"The *nembutsu* is an easy practice that anyone can do, no matter how ignorant or foolish or wicked he may be. All you have to do is say the *nembutsu*: *Namu Amida Butsu*,

Namu Amida Butsu, Namu Amida Butsu. If you recite the *nembutsu* like this, then when you die, you will surely go to the Pure Land. It is not I who say this, but Lord Amida himself who does. When Amida Buddha was in this world in the form of a prince named Hōzō Bodhisattva, he made forty-eight vows. The essential vow was the eighteenth, which said that anyone who recited *Namu Amida Butsu,* or "Hail Amida Buddha," would certainly attain rebirth in the Pure Land. This is called the Original Vow of Amida; and Hōzō Bodhisattva, after making his vows, endured all kinds of difficulties and austerities and in the end attained buddhahood. He became the Buddha Amida. That's why we can say that if you recite *Namu Amida Butsu,* you are certain to be reborn in Amida's Pure Land of Perfect Bliss. Lord Amida guarantees it. Lord Shakyamuni praises it. And remember that the holy Shan-tao of China tells us that the *nembutsu* is nothing other than the recitation, out loud, of the Holy Name, *Namu Amida Butsu.* So, my friends, let us believe Amida, believe Shakyamuni, and believe Shan-tao! If you believe these three, then your salvation is assured with the words *Namu Amida Butsu.* So, let's say the *nembutsu* now, together: *Namu Amida Butsu, Namu Amida Butsu.*"

When Hōnen began to recite the Holy Name, everyone joined in after him: *Namu Amida Butsu.* The recitation continued for a while until Hōnen broke off and began to speak again: "Now all of you can be certain of rebirth! But there are lots of people who disagree with my teachings, and I daresay there may be some among you who have doubts or questions about this Pure Land *nembutsu* doctrine. If you do have any doubts, feel free to ask."

One man put up his hand and began, "Most Reverend Hōnen, I understand that one can attain rebirth by reciting the *nembutsu;* but would it be better to recite in a very loud voice that can reach all the way to the Pure Land, so that

Lord Amida is sure to hear it? Or is it better to recite it to oneself so it can hardly be heard, since people say that the truest things are said in the lowest voices? What do you think about this?"

Hōnen replied with a smile, "If reciting in a loud voice ensured salvation, then crows and monkeys would be sure of Paradise. And if someone says it's best to say the *nembutsu* silently, then worms and octopuses would be the first to go to the Pure Land. What matters is not the size of your voice, but the purity and depth of your faith!"

Naozane thought the comparison with crows and monkeys and worms and octopuses very strange, but the crowd roared with laughter, clearly delighted with everything Hōnen was saying. Next, a voluptuous-looking woman raised her hand and asked a question: "Reverend sir, I am grateful to have learned the way of the *nembutsu* from you; but to my shame, I cannot forget the way of men and women—perhaps because of my sins in a former life. No matter how hard I try to give up the way of love and devote myself to the *nembutsu*, the image of the man I love keeps coming into my mind and breaking my concentration on the Holy Name. What am I to do?"

Having heard this question, the whole congregation turned as one to look at the woman. They all thought it only natural that a woman as attractive as she was could not forget the way of love. Everyone waited eagerly to see what kind of answer Hōnen would give to this particular question. Once again, he smiled: "Lovely lady, you seem to have a much heavier load of karma than most people. But Lord Amida has great love for people with heavy karmic burdens; he has said that he made his vows for them above all. If you can recite the *nembutsu* alone, do so; but if not sleeping with a man keeps you from reciting it, then say the *nembutsu* while in bed with your lover."

There was a great stir among the congregation at this reply, and it was evident that the people loved Hōnen from their hearts. "I hope this has resolved your doubts," he said. "Now, shall we all recite the *nembutsu* together?" The invocation began again, and grew louder and louder. As it did so, one voice in particular stood out, like the sound of a large, slightly cracked bell. It was the voice of Kumagai Naozane. He stood up, glared in Hōnen's direction, and shouted in a loud voice, "Reverend sir, reverend sir, I still have one question!" At this, the sound of the *nembutsu* ceased abruptly as everyone looked at Naozane. With shaggy hair and a bushy beard, he was a truly frightening-looking figure. Among the crowd, there were some who knew Naozane by sight. Soon, there were murmurs: "That is the famous Kumagai Naozane!" The murmurs grew louder until finally they reached Hōnen's ears.

"I have given up the life of a warrior for certain reasons, and I have one question to put to the holy monk Hōnen: can one truly go to the Pure Land of Perfect Bliss simply by reciting *Namu Amida Butsu*? That is my question."

As before, Hōnen smiled as he looked at Naozane and answered: "So you are Master Kumagai Jirō Naozane, who won fame for your valor at the battle of Ichinotani? I have heard much about you, and respect you as a great warrior. Now, as to your question: as I said earlier, if you will only recite the *nembutsu*, you can be reborn in Amida's Pure Land. It is certain."

"You really can?" asked Naozane again.

"Without question. Lord Amida has promised it; Lord Shakyamuni has guaranteed it; Master Shan-tao has stated it is certain. I cannot believe that these three holy ones are lying."

"*Namu Amida Butsu, Namu Amida Butsu, Namu Amida Butsu!*" Naozane suddenly began to recite the Holy Name.

"Now I've said the *nembutsu* three times—does that mean I can be reborn in the Pure Land?"

"Assuredly. Now you're a *nembutsu* devotee, and you will certainly go to the Pure Land of Perfect Bliss," answered Hōnen.

At this, Naozane burst into loud sobs. It was a strange sight: this strong, fierce-looking warrior breaking down and crying, with great tears running down his face. After he had wept unashamedly for a little while, he wiped away his tears and said, "I thought it would be a very hard thing to gain rebirth in Paradise, more difficult than destroying the Heike camp. I was ready to give one or two limbs, or even my life, to gain it. That was how I felt when I came here. And to think that I can get to Paradise without giving up my life, or even an arm or a leg, just by saying *Namu Amida Butsu!* I'm grateful, so grateful, so very grateful." And he started to cry again.

Hōnen sat watching him for a while and then, apparently deciding that this fine fellow would make a good disciple, admitted him to the community. This was how Naozane became a *nembutsu* monk.

Even after he returned to the Eastlands to spread the teachings, Naozane frequently recalled Hōnen's words when he admitted him to the community. True, the Master had said that anyone could go to the Pure Land if he simply recited the *nembutsu*. But Rensei-bō (as he was now called) often wondered if this might not be just a means of encouraging foolish and ignorant people to enter the way of the *nembutsu*. He read the *Sutra of Meditation on the Buddha of Infinite Life* and learned the doctrine of the nine grades of rebirth: the idea that, depending on their deeds in this life, *nembutsu* believers would be reborn in one of nine levels of the Pure Land, ranging from the "highest birth of the highest grade" down to the "lowest birth of the lowest grade."

Rensei-bō suspected that when Hōnen said everyone could be reborn, he meant at least in the lowest of the nine grades. Probably ordinary people could not attain rebirth on the higher levels, and particularly in the "highest birth of the highest grade." After all, it was said that the High Priest Eshin himself had prayed only for the "highest birth of the lowest grade." But Rensei-bō would never be content with that: if he was to be reborn, he wanted it to be on the highest level of all.

He had a particular reason for wanting this. There were frequent debates among Hōnen's disciples as to what became of people after their rebirth in the Pure Land. Did they simply remain there forever, or did they at some point come back to this world? It was a difficult question, and one day Rensei-bō had asked Hōnen himself about it.

"I don't really know what happens after rebirth, but I believe we come back. I don't see how a *nembutsu* believer could remain idly in the Pure Land as long as there are people still suffering in this world. When I come back, I'd like to have greater powers, so I could save as many of the suffering as possible."

Hearing this reply, Rensei-bō felt that he too would like to come back to this world and be able to save people as he wished, just like Hōnen. To do that, he would need to attain rebirth on the very highest level. He thought so at the time, and he became even more obsessed with the idea after going back to the East. He wanted to attain the highest birth of the highest grade; if he could not have that, he would just as soon be rejected altogether! He would make a vow, a powerful vow like Hōzō Bodhisattva's. And so he wrote a short hymn, expressing his personal vow:

The eight low levels of rebirth
I now forsake, nor for them shall I pray.

For those who pass into those realms
Cannot return again one day.

Having made his vow, Rensei-bō prayed daily to Lord Amida that it might be fulfilled.

One night about a month after making his vow, he had a dream. There was a large pond whose surface was covered with lotus flowers. The flowers were of many colors, red and blue and purple, as well as the white ones usual in this world. They grew in such rich and wild profusion that the pond was filled with them; but in their very midst, there rose a single huge lotus stem. It was as thick as a cryptomeria tree, and towered up over a hundred feet. At the tip of that tall, thick trunk shone a golden lotus which gave off a wondrous fragrance.

"This is the lotus for those who attain the highest birth of the highest grade," a voice whispered. Rensei-bō was one among tens of thousands of onlookers gathered around the pond. Everyone was drinking wine, eating dainties, and waiting in anticipation of a spectacle which was just about to begin.

A warrior in armor leapt into the pond and at once swam his way to the lotus stem. He began to climb up slowly, but it was so slippery that there was hardly a hand- or foot-hold for him. Even so, the armored warrior hung on frantically and kept climbing. It was hard for him, though—perhaps due to the weight of his armor. The pace at which he climbed grew slower and slower, until at last he slipped from the stem and fell into the pond.

Then another man swam lightly across the pond and arrived at the lotus stem. He climbed up it, deft as a monkey, to the amazement of the crowd. "Oh, that's the acrobat from China," said someone. The acrobat had soon climbed to a point just below the golden lotus, but to get on top of the flower he would have to make his way up from under the open petals. These petals, however, were of an almost metallic hardness. The acrobat did his best to clamber up their undersides so as to emerge on top, but it was a far more difficult task than scaling the stem had been. It proved impossible even for him, and he too fell into the pond.

The onlookers' sighs ruffled the surface of the water. Then, as if in mockery, a long-nosed goblin used a fan of feathers to rise through the air high up into the sky. "An Indian goblin!" cried the crowd, though Rensei-bō did not know how they could tell—it was little different from an ordinary Japanese goblin. Waving the fan, it balanced skillfully, moving up and down, right and left, positioning itself just over the lotus. All it had to do now was descend and make its landing. Just when the crowd was sure it would succeed, there was a roll of thunder and a flash of lightning, and the goblin was nowhere to be seen. "It's against the rules. We can't have that! The rule is that you *swim* across the pond and *climb* up the trunk!" said someone.

For some time thereafter, no one attempted to approach the lotus, but eventually a warrior appeared and announced loudly: "I am Rensei-bō of Kumagai, Master Hōnen's most-favored disciple, and I shall be the first to mount the lotus of the highest birth of the highest grade!"

The figure was certainly Rensei-bō, but another Rensei-bō was standing by the pond, watching him. This second Rensei-bō looking on anxiously as the first one slowly breast-stroked his way toward the lotus stem and, reaching it, began to climb steadily upward. When he came to the point just below the opened flower, he drew his sword and cut a hole in the petals, and thus was able to climb up onto the lotus. Then he cried out proudly, in a voice like a cracked bell, "I, Rensei-bō of Kumagai, am the first one to attain the highest birth of the highest grade in the Pure Land of

Perfect Bliss!" The watching crowd burst into loud cheers, and the second Rensei-bō standing by the side of the pond also cheered and applauded. The loud sound of the applause, in fact, woke Rensei-bō from his dream.

The people of those days believed in dream-oracles, in which the gods and buddhas revealed their will in the form of dreams. Thus it was not unreasonable for Rensei-bō to think that Lord Amida had given him a personal guarantee of the highest birth in the highest grade of Paradise in the form of this dream.

Rensei-bō boasted to his family and his students, "I'm sure to be reborn in the highest level of Paradise. Lord Amida told me so in a dream. I'm sure Master Hōnen will be able to too, but I'll get there first!"

"Well, that's wonderful, isn't it," those around him said; but they were hard put to find a good response to his next announcement.

"Now then, since my rebirth in the highest grade is guaranteed, I want to get to Paradise as soon as I can. And I'd like as many people as possible to watch me when I do it."

"Oh, but there's no need to rush it, surely," they said.

"No, no. 'Hasten to do a good deed,' as the proverb says."

"Well, but, it's not so easy, dying. Are you planning to perform *harakiri?*"

"Of course not. I have no intention whatsoever of cutting my belly open. I've been praying to Lord Amida every day, and I'm sure he'll come and get me himself when the time comes."

His family and students tried to persuade Rensei-bō to give up this reckless plan of his, but he was the sort who, once he got an idea in his head, would listen to no one. There was nothing for it but to go along with his plan, worrisome though that was. He despatched his students to all areas of the Eastlands, having them put up signs at the street corners announcing his intention of publicly accomplishing his rebirth in the Pure Land: "On the fifteenth day of the second month of next year, Rensei-bō of Kumagai will carry out his vow to attain the highest birth of the highest grade in the Pure Land of Perfect Bliss. Let all who doubt this come and see for themselves. Come and witness Kumagai's end, and recount it for generation after generation."

It was in the ninth month of the previous year that Rensei-bō had his students put these signs up. In the succeeding months, a great many people read them and decided to see for themselves the journey to Paradise of Kumagai Rensei-bō, the greatest hero of the Eastlands. When the time came, huge crowds gathered in Kumagai village, the numbers reaching into the tens and hundreds of thousands.

A clay platform, rather like a large sumo ring, had been built in the middle of a broad plain, at Rensei-bō's orders. There was a square lower section and a round stage-like area above. A large number of monks were seated in the lower section and had been reciting the *nembutsu* since morning. At last, a little past noon, Rensei-bō made his entrance, preceded and followed by an attendant monk. He seated himself on the round upper stage and began to read, together with the other monks, the three principal sutras sacred to the Pure Land School. When they finished, the invocation of the Holy Name began. The plan was that Lord Amida would come to welcome him and escort him to the Pure Land during the invocations.

Since it was all planned in advance, Rensei-bō had no doubts about what would happen: in the midst of the chanted *nembutsu*, he would hear the music of the heavenly maidens and would see Lord Amida, accompanied by the bodhisattvas Kannon and Seishi, coming to welcome him. They would invite him to mount a lotus-throne and then waft him to paradise.

Actually, he had been quite concerned about the events of this day ever since he had announced his impending rebirth to the public in the ninth month of the previous year. He had inquired of Lord Amida many times if everything was in order. Each time, the Buddha had smiled warmly and said nothing. Rensei-bō had interpreted this to mean that everything was set. After all, why would Lord Amida not grant the wish of someone who reverenced him and yearned for his Pure Land so deeply?

The *nembutsu* recitation had begun, and the crowd was waiting in breathless anticipation to watch Rensei-bō go to Paradise. But no strains of sacred music played by heavenly maidens came to Rensei-bō's ears. And no trace of Lord Amida coming to welcome him at the head of the Holy Throng was visible. What had happened, he wondered. He put his hand to his chest and found that his heart was still beating with perfect regularity. His body was still filled with the life force. At this rate, he'd never die! He had no choice but to call off his rebirth.

"I have an announcement to make to all of you who were good enough to come from the distant parts of the Eastlands to witness how I, Rensei-bō, would attain rebirth. I am truly sorry to have put you to so much trouble today, and I am very grateful to you all. I had planned to leave for Paradise here and now, but I have just received a message from Lord Amida saying that he is very busy in the Pure Land today and will not be able to come for me. Of course, he could have sent Kannon and Seishi as his representatives, but he feels he has to come himself in a case like mine, where it's the highest birth of the highest grade. That's what he said. So my rebirth will be postponed until the fourth day of the ninth month, next year. I ask you all to come back then, when you'll be able to see Kumagai Naozane ascend in glory to Paradise." This was said in a voice which, though fully audible to the congregation, was not nearly as loud as usual.

The crowd was amazed, and also disappointed, like an audience that has come to see a famous actor perform and then finds the play canceled. Tens of thousands, hundreds of thousands of sighs escaped from as many mouths. Then the sighs changed to mocking laughter, and at last to jeers. "Shitty priest—afraid to die, are you?" "Swindler! You lied to get us here so you could take our money!" The crowd left the village of Kumagai in a storm of complaints and insults.

Rensei-bō's family and students had lost face and were painfully troubled by the question of why he hadn't decided to carry out his plan. All he could do was humbly apologize to them: "I'm sorry, very sorry. I shouldn't have trusted Lord Amida so much."

His failure to attain rebirth was a great shock to Rensei-bō. He had been disgraced in front of a crowd of tens and hundreds of thousands. Nothing was more unbearable to an Eastern warrior than public disgrace—the only recourse was to die. But he had planned to die and then failed, the ultimate shame. He had to do something to clear his name: he absolutely had to succeed in attaining rebirth on the fourth day of the ninth month, next year.

Meeting with humiliation for the first time in his life, he began to reflect deeply on himself, also for the first time. It had been wrong of him not to make sure he understood Lord Amida's intentions; wrong to interpret them as he saw fit, according to his own convenience. He realized that now. He was sixty-seven years old but in perfect physical health. His body was that of a young man. He knew that rebirth would be very difficult for him unless he somehow weakened his strong body and also his spirit, teaching it meekness. And that is just what he now set out to do.

He still had a year and a half, time enough in which to tame body and spirit and make them ready for Lord Amida's coming. He would first have to cut back on his food. He had been a big eater since his youth, and a big drinker as well. Drinking had been given up as a matter of course when he became a monk, but he was still a big eater. He would polish off five bowls of rice as well as double portions of meat, fish, and vegetables at a single meal. This was hardly preparation for death! He decided to take only one portion of rice and one bowl of soup each day. This total reversal of the habits of many years was almost as painful as dying.

Nevertheless he rigorously observed the precepts he had set for himself, and his efforts were highly successful. After half a year, he had grown very thin; and in another year he was so weak that it was painful for him to be out of bed. Watching him, his family and students worried whether he could last until the fourth day of the ninth month. If he died before then, it would simply compound the disgrace. Yet Rensei-bō did last, despite their fears. All summer he had kept to his bed, but as the appointed date approached, he got up and set to work with his students, practicing and preparing for the long-awaited day.

At last it came. This time a dry riverbed had been chosen as the site, and people gathered from all over the Eastlands and even other parts of Japan—if not in as great numbers as before, at any rate in the tens of thousands. The student-monks had been chanting the *nembutsu* there since early morning when, shortly after noon, Rensei-bō, accompanied by two attendants, joined them. He was dressed in a ragged black cassock, rather than the rich golden vestments he had worn the year before. The year and a half of ascetic living had left him terribly thin; everyone was amazed to see the mighty Rensei-bō turned to skin and bones. Only his piercing eyes were unchanged, reminding them of the former Kumagai Jirō Naozane.

He sat down on the crude straw mat spread on the river-bed and joined his companions in reciting the Holy Name. He did not read the *Three Sutras*, as before, but began at once with the simple repetition of the *nembutsu*. He had hardly begun to recite it when he heard from somewhere the faint sound of beautiful music. The music of the heavenly maidens! he thought, and then saw Amida Buddha with Kannon and Seishi in the midst of the Holy Throng coming to welcome him. Lord Amida spoke: "You have been a pure-hearted believer in the *nembutsu*. And so, Rensei-bō, I will take you now to my Pure Land of Perfect Bliss, for the highest birth of the highest grade."

Hearing Amida's voice, Rensei-bō was assured at last that he had attained his goal. Looking at the Buddha's face, he noticed that it seemed strangely like Master Hōnen's. He gave a little gasp of surprise, and with that he was gone.

One of the student-monks felt his pulse and, telling the crowd by signs that he was dead, asked them all to join in the *nembutsu*. The invocation of the Holy Name rising from tens of thousands of throats echoed to the heavens and pierced the earth, praising the wondrous rebirth of this peerless devotee of the *nembutsu*.

How the Gods Came to Kumano

Thank you all very much for visiting this humble shrine. And now I would like to tell you about the gods of Kumano, whose shrines you will be visiting. There are three principal deities here: the gods of Nachi, the Original Shrine, and the New Shrine. I'm going to tell you how these deities came to be here. The basic idea is that all of the gods of Japan were originally Indian buddhas and bodhisattvas who showed themselves in temporary forms here. I'm not really sure why the buddhas wanted to take the form of Japanese gods, but it seems they did; and the god of Nachi is a manifestation of the Eleven-headed Kannon; the god of the New Shrine, of Yakushi Buddha; and the god of the Original Shrine, of Amida Buddha.

These three buddhas—Kannon, Yakushi, and Amida—were, it's said, originally human beings. The Chinese character for buddha is written "not-human"; but this doesn't mean that they were *never* human. Rather, they are *transformed* human beings. Now I'm sure you all think that only very virtuous people become buddhas, but that's not necessarily true. People who've lived eccentric lives and those with a heavy weight of karma can become buddhas too.

Just when it was, I'm not sure, but there was a country in India called Magadha. The capital of the country was a great city. They say it took five days to go from the eastern to the western edges, and seven days to go from the northern to the southern edges of it. It was a huge place, even by comparison with our great capital of Heian-kyō. And since we are told that the roads running north and south were paved with gold, and those running east and west with silver, it must have been awfully rich too.

Now in this land there were ten thousand ministers of state, fifty thousand noblemen, one hundred thousand courtiers, and one thousand royal consorts. The neighboring country of China did not have as many as ten thousand ministers, but it did have three thousand royal consorts. In the case of Magadha, the number of consorts seems a little small to me in comparison with the number of ministers. But even so, it must have been very hard to have one thousand wives at once. Even though the king was attended by these one thousand wives, for some reason no child was born. Still, he was so busy with governmental affairs, and love affairs, that he hardly noticed the loneliness that comes from being childless. Then one day, everything changed.

A pair of little birds were feeding their young, the male and the female taking turns to get the food and put it into their babies' mouths. Watching them, the king said, "That pair of birds, husband and wife, look so happy! Through what chain of karma have they found this happiness, while I have not? I have a thousand wives, and if each of them bore just one child, I would have a thousand children. And yet I don't have a single one—what an unhappy man I am!"

Neither the ministers of state nor the royal consorts had

anything to say to this, but a priest who happened to be there replied as follows: "Your Majesty's seed is so noble that it cannot easily form a child within the body of a woman. Yet among your thousand consorts, I am sure there is one who can receive your seed fruitfully. Just as one in a thousand persons is like a buddha, so too, one of your wives will be able to accept your noble seed and bear you a splendid, princely son. Therefore I beg Your Majesty to make the rounds of your consorts even more assiduously than up to now and endeavor with the utmost care to father a child."

This was a very wise suggestion on the part of the priest.

He suspected that if the king did not have a child as yet, it was because he was overtaxing himself with his thousand wives. How clever it was of him to say that such noble seed does not easily bear fruit! And his advice to "make the rounds more assiduously" was also in his own interest, for even if the king visited one wife each day, it would take three years to visit them all. Thus, the priest's irresponsible lie would not be revealed for quite some time.

The priest's words caused the king to reconsider his marital arrangements. Governance was of great importance to him, of course, but the part of his life centered on the women's quarters of the palace was just as important. Behind each of his thousand wives, there were ministers and noblemen who were fathers or elder brothers. If he neglected to show his affection to even one of his consorts, her resentment would breed anger in her male relatives, and this in turn would endanger the king's conduct of government. He needed to make love to all his wives with complete impartiality, and had devised a schedule including three hundred of them each year.

But he had to treat with special care the daughters and younger sisters of the most powerful men. Them, he needed to make love to ten or twenty times a year. As a result, he began to neglect his three-hundred-per-year plan, and more and more cut corners. Now the priest's words had made the king reflect carefully on his work of the past few years. He decided from that day forward to make love to one wife a day, doing his best for each one without distinction.

Among his wives was a lady called Senkuho, the daughter of a man named Kensaishō. (I don't know what characters you'd use to write these odd-sounding names, unlearned person that I am, but those are the names that have been handed down for centuries.) The lady was not exceptionally beautiful, but she had a charming plumpness and looked like the type who would be very much blessed with children. She was calm and gentle, and a pious believer in the Buddha's teachings.

The king hardly noticed this quiet, not particularly beautiful lady among his thousand consorts, and his conjugal visit, which should have come 'round once every three and a half years, was completely omitted twice in a row. As a result, the lady's chamber remained empty for seven or eight years. She prayed constantly to the Eleven-headed Kannon that the king's love might be turned toward her. Perhaps that was why one night, following the priest's advice to make sure to visit each and every wife, the king came to the lady's quarters for a leisurely and passionate visit.

For some reason the king was very taken with this lady and began to spend all his time with her. The other ladies were angry and resentful, and the ministers were shocked, since the king had never before acted so arbitrarily. The king, however, didn't seem to care about the other wives' anger or sorrow or his ministers' shock and suspicion—he continued to stay with her. He began saying things like, "I've met a buddha! I never realized there were buddhas like this hidden among ordinary people. What a fool I've been!" Such statements made the other wives even angrier, and the ministers tried to remonstrate with the king, but he wouldn't listen.

Why did the king become so very fond of this particular wife? The meddlesome courtiers had several theories—for instance, that if a woman like that, of no particular beauty, had been able to win the king's heart, it must be because she had some hidden physical charm that turned him to jelly. And what a fuss they made about it! Why is it that men, in particular, are so fond of gossip of this sort? I myself, as a nun in service to the Buddha, know nothing of such things. "Oh, yes? You look quite well versed in the ways of love, Sister," some of you are thinking. Well, don't! I *live* to serve the Buddha. I'm still a pure maiden without experience of men.

Anyway, the king continued to stay with Lady Senkuho and built her a splendid palace. It was called the Gosuiten Palace, and she became known in turn as Lady Gosuiten. In time, Lady Gosuiten showed signs of being with child. The king was exceedingly pleased at this wonderful news, but the other nine hundred and ninety-nine wives were not very happy, as you might expect. Women, you see (and not just lowly ones like me, but even the highest of the high), cannot escape the sin of jealousy. The nine hundred and ninety-nine ladies gathered in one place and, consumed with jealousy and envy, talked about her: "Lady Gosuiten *says* she's carrying the king's child, but it must be a lie. It's the lot of women to bear children, but it's incredible that a base person like her could be with child when we nine hundred and ninety-nine others could not. No doubt she wanted the king's child so badly that she took herself off in secret to some stable-boy or sumo wrestler somewhere and got herself pregnant. Now she claims it's the king's seed! If he failed to get any one of us nine hundred and ninety-nine ladies with child, it's because he *has* no seed. He's a seedless watermelon! Can a seedless watermelon bear fruit? The seed she's carrying isn't watermelon seed, it's—*bumpkin* seed!"

They carried on like this, pouring out insults and abuse to make themselves feel better. Then one of them called Lady Renge had an idea: "It may be the child of a stableboy or a wrestler, but if it's born of a lady whom the king is consorting with, it will become the king's son. What's the point in spouting insults? It would be better to curse the child and make it die."

The other ladies all agreed and summoned a priest famed for his great magical powers. "Don't let the child Lady Gosuiten is carrying be born in the world of men: turn it into a wild animal. Or, let it be flushed away with the waste water." For seven days and seven nights they had him cast his spells, but to no effect.

Then the nine hundred and ninety-nine wives gathered together again to take counsel. The gods and buddhas, it appeared, would not listen to their pleas. But in the next country there lived a skillful soothsayer. They decided to send a messenger and summon him. When he arrived at the palace, the ladies told him, "Lady Gosuiten is said to be with child. We hear you can divine someone's past for forty years back and their future for forty years forward. Will this child be male or female, a human or a beast? And what will its destiny be? Tell us!"

The soothsayer shook his divining rods for a while and then read them. With a bright smile he announced to the royal consorts: "This is indeed a good omen! The child her ladyship is carrying will be a boy, a prince. From the day of his birth, the people will be free from tribulations, and the land will be at peace. At the age of three, he will be made crown prince, and at seven he will ascend the throne as king. During his reign the land of Magadha will extend its sway beyond its borders and enjoy great prosperity."

The nine hundred and ninety-nine ladies gave him angry looks. "You may be a famous soothsayer, but you know nothing about a woman's feelings! Couldn't you tell that we did *not* want an answer like that?"

At this, the soothsayer assumed a more dignified posture and replied, "That is what the omens say. I have simply explained them to you as they are. It is said that if you tell something contrary to what the omens say, you will be cursed by the god of divination and fall into the hells—you and your descendants unto the seventh generation."

"Fall into the hells unto the seventh generation? Don't be ridiculous! We know lots of soothsayers who tell lies, and they are alive and well, and so are their children. A really good soothsayer is the one who reads his client's mind and tells her what she wants to hear. Now, we'd like you to give the king a reading, and tell him precisely what we say. We'll make you rich if you do. We'll give you fine robes to wear. We'll even let you have our bodies for your pleasure. Wouldn't you like to have a taste of nine hundred and ninety-nine beautiful women, all still young and fresh? And if by any chance you should tell the king anything close to what you've said to us just now, we nine hundred and ninety-nine ladies will join together to curse you. We'll send you to the very worst, limitless hell—you and your descendants unto the seventh generation!" They laughed horribly.

That's what the royal consorts told the poor soothsayer, and how terrifying their voices were! Now, the soothsayer had a wife who had, ten years earlier, found him out in just one infidelity. What an uproar! Perhaps his wife was twice as jealous as the average woman—anyway, she seemed to go quite mad. Even now he approached her with the utmost care. So he was well aware that even one woman could easily send a man to hell; and he had no doubt at all that if he were cursed by nine hundred and ninety-nine, it would mean limitless hell for seven generations. Naturally he replied, "I will do as your ladyships wish in all things. What precisely shall I tell his majesty?"

There was a total change in the ladies' attitudes. "Oh, wonderful, wonderful! You *are* a fine soothsayer," they told him in gentle voices. "Tell the king this: the child the Lady Gosuiten is carrying will be a very wicked prince; and when he is three years of age, a great calamity will come upon our land and wipe out the ministers of state, the nobility, and most of the common people. Then when he is seven, the king himself will lose his life. . . . Tell the king that."

A few days later, the nine hundred and ninety-nine ladies went to the king and said, "We're sure the child who is to be born will be a male, a prince; and we suggest your majesty consult a soothsayer about his future. In the neighboring land there is a famous diviner who can see forty years into the past and future alike. Why don't you ask him about the prince?"

"All right," nodded the king. "I'll summon him and have him tell my son's fortune." And so the man was brought before the king and said precisely what the nine hundred and ninety-nine ladies had told him to say. The soothsayer feared (and the ladies dearly hoped) that the king would become enraged when he heard this prediction. But he simply said, "I see . . . a bad king, eh? You say my son will be an exceptionally bad king? That'd be all right! You have to be pretty bad to handle a big country like this. A good man'd be made a fool of by the neighboring kings. After all, the great King Ajase who enlarged our domains in former times seems to have been a very bad king indeed—killing his father and imprisoning his mother. Now, I may *look* like a good king, but underneath I'm quite a bad one myself. The king of a great country should let people think him a good man but should on no account *be* one. So it's good if the prince becomes a 'bad' king. And you say I'd only have seven more years to live? That's all right with me, if I can experience a father's joy in having a son for a full seven years."

Some days later, the nine hundred and ninety-nine royal consorts gathered again to have a talk: "Despite the king's brave words, he's unsettled in mind about the prince. One more little push from us should do the trick." They devised a plan: each of them would search the land of Magadha for the oldest, most fearsome-looking hag she could find. They would dress the old women in red, put drums and fifes and other noise-makers in their hands, and have them push their way into the Gosuiten Palace, where the king was staying.

When the day came, the nine hundred and ninety-nine old women sounded their noise-makers and howled out, "The one thousand hags of heaven do now present themselves at the palace of Lady Gosuiten. The Lord of heaven has heard that her ladyship has conceived a future evil king, and he commands that the wicked child be killed in the womb, and its head brought to him. He also said we may take the lives of its mother, Lady Gosuiten, and its father, his majesty the king." They tittered and sniggered. "We'll escort you all to heaven before tomorrow dawns!" Their weird voices resounded in the darkness, making the hair of those who heard them stand on end.

The king had given a bold response to the soothsayer's prediction a few days before, but in fact he felt uneasy. And now, seeing these one thousand hags appear in the palace in the middle of the night, it was not surprising that he would be shaken, and wonder if he should have taken the diviner's words more seriously. "Heavens! You must be possessed by an unlucky spirit," he said to Lady Gosuiten. "I just remembered, I have some business to attend to so I must return to my own palace." And so he did.

The Lady, left to herself, reflected sadly that the king, on whom she totally depended, had seemed so frightened that he would almost certainly never come to her again.

The nine hundred and ninety-nine wives met and boasted to one another about how well everything had gone, and what a wonderful plan it was. They knew, though, that eventually the Lady would discover it had all been their doing— the soothsayer, the old hags, everything. It would be necessary, then, to get her out of the way before she found out. And so they devised another terrifying stratagem. They would forge a royal proclamation and use it to have seven soldiers come and take Lady Gosuiten far off into the mountains, where they would kill her. The ladies bribed the ministers of state to issue the false proclamation directly to the soldiers in the king's name. Naturally, the soldiers thought it was a genuine royal command.

Their instructions were to take Lady Gosuiten to the foot of Mount Chikoshakuō, a seven-day march to the south of the capital, and there to cut off her head. They proceeded to the lady's palace and read out the proclamation in a very loud voice. The men and women attendants who were there hurriedly packed their things (and not only *their* things, but the Lady Gosuiten's as well) and began pushing and shoving each other aside to make their getaways. The Lady had heard that at times like this men's hearts were not to be relied upon; and now, watching her people and even the dogs and cats flee pell-mell from the palace, she keenly felt the meanness of the human heart.

The soldiers too felt sad at this demonstration of men's selfishness, and were very sorry for the Lady, who was left all alone. But they had their job to do, and time pressed. Urging the Lady on, they left the palace and set out on the seven-day march to Mount Chikoshakuō. A seven-day journey on foot was very painful for the Lady, who had seldom ventured outside the palace. It was sad to see blisters forming on her jewel-like feet and then bleeding as the march went on. When at last they arrived at the foot of the mountain, the soldiers said, "Your ladyship, traveling with you, we have all come to have deep respect for your character. We would save you if we could, but since it is by order of the king himself there is nothing we can do. So please, your ladyship, have pity on us and allow us to take your head."

"Of course," she replied with a gentle smile, "I am quite resigned to death. Only, I would like to be allowed to recite the sutras a bit before I die." Naturally the soldiers had no objection to this, so the Lady took from the folds of her dress a small image of Kannon, the bodhisattva of mercy, and placing it on a rock, began to pray: "O merciful Kannon, I have always trusted in you; now help me, I pray. I don't care about my own life, but I must somehow save the king's seed that lives within me. And so I ask you to spare my life until I can bear my child."

When she had finished praying, she spoke to the soldiers: "I have prayed earnestly to the Buddha and I'm sure he will take me to his Pure Land. Please behead me quickly and let me go to Paradise." Then, sitting in formal posture, she bent her head and exposed her neck to the executioners. They hesitated to take her life, but there was nothing they could do. The soldier who was to do the beheading came up behind her, raised his sword high, and, with a cry, brought it down hard. Now it was a very sharp sword, the lightest stroke of which should have sent any head flying; but for some reason, when he brought it down on Lady Gosuiten's neck, it sprang back, as if it had struck stone, and the blade shattered into pieces. The soldiers were stunned, and one after another they tried their own swords on the Lady's neck. But it seemed to have turned to the hardest of stone, and the swords kept breaking and the blades shattering.

The soldiers looked at each other in amazement and began to discuss something in low voices, but the Lady said, "It's Kannon saving me, I'm sure of it. He's made my neck as hard as stone until the day I give birth to my child. Won't you please wait until then to kill me?" The soldiers had little choice but to do as she asked.

After a time, the Lady gave birth to a jewel-like prince. The soldiers supposed that her neck should now have returned from its stone-like hardness before the birth to normal soft flesh. They urged the Lady to prepare herself and were about to cut off her head when she asked once again if she could say a final prayer to Kannon. "O holy Kannon, I beg that, even though my head be separated from my body, my breasts might remain uncorrupted and continue to give good milk for three years, to provide food for my son. And I ask that you have the tigers and wolves and foxes and serpents on this mountain protect my son, and have no thoughts of harming him."

When she finished this prayer, the Lady extended her soft white neck. "Now then, please behead me," she said. One of the soldiers brought his sword down, crying *"Namu Amida Butsu!"* The Lady's head fell from her shoulders and rolled about on the ground as the new-born prince lying nearby cried and screamed.

The soldiers, taking advantage of the fact that the proclamation said nothing about killing the child, left him as he was, simply putting the Lady's head in a sack and taking it back with them. "The child will die soon enough. May the tigers and wolves and foxes and serpents on this mountain guard his life for a while!" they said as they left.

And so the little prince was left by himself beside the headless body of his mother. Naturally he sought his mother's milk; and, strange to tell, the mother's full breasts continued to drip sweet-tasting milk into his mouth, just as if she were still alive. This continued for ten days, then twenty; then one, two, and three months. The head was gone, and the flesh of the body from the waist down gradually fell away until, after three months, only white bones were left. The torso alone remained as it had been, the ample breasts like a never-failing spring constantly dripping fresh, sweet milk into the prince's mouth. This was how the child was able to survive for ten days, then twenty; one month, then three.

And this was not all. The tigers and wolves, foxes and serpents, far from harming the prince, brought leaves and grasses and laid them over him to shield him from the cold. The tigresses and she-wolves sometimes cuddled him and gently licked his body as they would their own young. And so the little prince survived for three full years.

Lady Gosuiten had before her death begged Kannon to work this miracle for her son for a period of three years. If he had mother's milk for that long, she was sure he could grow up strong and healthy; and she was determined on that. But now those three years were almost up. The mountain beasts were wondering when to tell the prince; they knew he would be downcast at the news, and hesitated to give it to him. At last only three days were left. The animals asked a certain fox who was good friends with the prince and was working hard at teaching him human speech to break the news. The fox didn't much like this task, but someone had to do it, so he said to the child (who looked very contented after having drunk his fill of mother's milk): "It's about time you stopped taking that milk. We foxes only drink it for three months, and even humans stop after a year or so. But you're still guzzling away after three years! You'd better stop. You're the only human child in the forest. Do you know who your parents were? Actually, you know—now don't fall over— you're the son of the king of Magadha! And your mother was called Lady Gosuiten—

she was one of the king's thousand wives. The king showed her special favor, and that's how she came to carry you inside her. But the nine hundred and ninety-nine other wives were very jealous of her: they tricked her into letting herself be taken to the foot of this mountain, where she was killed.

"We animals on the mountain remember exactly what happened three years ago. The Lady prayed to Kannon before she died, 'At least let my breasts remain alive so my child can have milk.' She also asked us animals to look after you—I can still hear the sadness in her voice when she spoke. And that's why the animals of the forest were so kind to you; even the fierce tigers and wolves loved you like one of their own cubs. It was because they were moved by the sad, gentle heart of your mother. But remember, Prince, that the three years are up in just three days!"

Though the prince had realized that he himself was a human being living in the midst of the animals, he had never worried about who his father or mother might be. The animals tried to avoid touching on the matter; it seemed to be something the prince should not ask about. It was as if there were some deep dark secret hidden away somewhere. He was afraid to ask, and never did.

Now, however, he had unexpectedly learned from the fox the secret of his birth. It was a great shock to him, but even greater was the sorrow he felt at soon having to part from his mother's breasts. He began to wail in a loud voice. His grief was so intense that the fox regretted having said anything, and tried to console him: "It's that painful for you to be separated from your mother's breasts, is it? Well, it's no wonder, since you've thought of them as your real mother all this time. But nothing that lives can escape the fate of dying. Men, tigers, wolves, foxes, serpents—they all die. That lovely flower over there will wilt, and that tree will wither. It's the destiny of all living things. Shakyamuni Buddha called it 'the truth that all things are impermanent.' We animals know all about the truth of impermanence even without hearing the Buddha preach. All that has life must die, and everything with form will be broken. Your mother's life-breath is long gone, but her attachment to you survives, in the form of those breasts. In another three days, though, even the breasts will wither. It is the way of this world."

Despite these wise words, the prince continued to cry. He cried for three days and three nights, without eating or drinking anything.

When the appointed day came, the animals gathered before the breasts of Lady Gosuiten, making offerings of food and water, and praying to them as if to the gods and buddhas themselves. At just around noon, the very time the Lady's head had been struck from her shoulders, there came the sound of lovely music, like a funerary song. The animals stood startled for a while, listening intently to the sounds, and then the breasts began slowly to vanish like light snow melting in the warm spring sunshine. The animals watched it happen, holding their breath as the white, white breasts grew gradually smaller and then completely disappeared. Unlike the snow in spring, there was not a single drop of moisture left behind; all that remained were some white bones.

There were some among the animals who simply could not believe the marvel they had seen. "We *thought* there was a pair of breasts there, but probably it was just a delusion," they said. And indeed it may have been, because it's impossible that Lady Gosuiten should have died and her breasts survived. On the other hand, those breasts did certainly give milk to the little prince for three whole years, thus keeping him alive. So how could it be a delusion? The animals discussed the matter from several points of view.

The prince had watched as if in a dream his mother's breasts melt away like snow. He had already wept all his tears the other day, and the actual parting was not quite as painful as had been the experience of being told, three days before, that he must bid the breasts farewell forever.

The animals gathered Lady Gosuiten's bones in one spot and had a simple funeral. Then they began to discuss what to do with the prince. The wolf spoke first: "True, the prince is a human child, but he was born on this mountain. For the past three years he has been nourished at his mother's breasts, but we animals actually raised him. He's attached to us, and we love him like our own child or brother. He may be a human by nature, but we animals are the ones who nurtured him. He ought to stay here and live with us—that will make him happy, and us too."

Most of the animals gave loud shouts of joy to express their agreement with the wolf's speech. The tiger, however, had a different opinion: "The wolf's view has something to be said for it. The prince is a good friend for us here in the forest, and he would become an even better friend as he grew up here. He'll turn into a strong young man, from whom much can be expected. It would naturally be good and pleasant for us to have such a strong, reliable friend. But the question is, would it be a good thing for the prince? He is, after all, a human child, and we should return him to his fellow humans. I think that would be best for him. I hear that the king has not been blessed with any more children and is very troubled at having no one to succeed him. He'll be overjoyed to learn that the prince is alive and well. I'm sure he'll want to leave his throne to his son. And what greater happiness could there be for a human being than to become a king? We'll miss him, of course, but we ought to return him to the world of men, and to his father the king."

As he spoke, large teardrops fell in a torrent from the tiger's big, fierce-looking eyes. Seeing his tears, the other animals all found themselves agreeing with the tiger's view and felt they must indeed return the prince to the human world and to the king, his father. They argued for a while about just how to do it, until they remembered the excellent Buddhist monk named Chiken whose temple stood at the foot of the mountain. Chiken was supposed to be on very good terms with the king, so he would be the best person of all to entrust with the prince. They decided to send the fox as messenger and have him escort the monk halfway up the mountainside, where they would hand over the prince.

One afternoon a few days later, as Chiken was reading in his room at the temple, a fox slipped in and started beckoning him. The monk's first thought was to drive the troublesome creature away, but no matter what he did, the fox showed no signs of leaving. It seemed to be trying to tell him to come along because it had something to show him. Finally Chiken decided to follow the fox, taking along three attendant monks. Coming to a spot in mid-mountain where there was a splendid view, he saw on the opposite slope a large crowd of animals, with a tiger in the lead. Recognizing the monk, the tiger addressed him in a loud voice: "You are the holy monk Chiken, are you not? The child you see here is in fact the son of the king of Magadha; his mother was a royal consort named Lady Gosuiten. She enjoyed the king's favor and conceived this prince, and for that reason was envied by the other nine hundred and ninety-nine wives, who had her brought to this mountain and beheaded. The prince's life was in great danger too, but we animals felt sorry for him and raised him here in the mountains for three years. But a human child should, after all, live among humans; so, holding back our tears, we wish to return him to the human world and to the king."

Chiken could tell that the tiger was struggling to keep from crying, and wondered at the strange things that occur in this world. "Fine, fine," he said. "It was good of you to care for the child. I thank you sincerely on behalf of the king. And I promise that we'll make a splendid prince of the boy!"

No sooner had he finished speaking than a wolf took the boy on his back and sped like an arrow down the valley, right to where the monk stood waiting. Chiken took the boy back to his temple, saying nothing about the matter to anyone else. He knew it was too early to introduce the child to the king: it would be best to teach him proper human manners and supply him with a little learning first. And so the monk applied himself to the task of teaching the prince the manners needed in human society—no easy job in the case of a boy who'd been raised among wolves and tigers. But the monk's efforts paid off, and the prince was soon a decently mannered little boy. He was also very apt at studies, and by the age of five or six could read quite difficult books. Chiken tried to teach the prince both "internal studies," that is, Buddhism, and "external studies," or non-Buddhist learning; but the prince was interested only in the former sort. The Buddhist teaching that "All who live must die, and all who meet are fated to part" seemed to appeal to him especially. "That's the way the world really is," he would say.

Four years passed in this way until the prince reached the age of seven. He had turned into a handsome lad who looked just like his father the king. Observing how much promise he showed, Chiken was immensely pleased. "I've raised you for four years now," he told him one day. "There was more than a touch of the woods about you at first; but you've managed to learn how human beings are supposed to behave, and you've made wonderful progress in your studies for a boy of your age. I think it's time we showed you to the king—how about it?"

Naturally the prince had no objection to this, and so one day the eminent monk took the little prince to the palace. The king glanced at the boy and said to Chiken, "It's been a long time, reverend sir! Even when I invite you, you rarely come; but today some good wind has blown you our way, it seems. I am very pleased. With your spiritual powers, you can bring peace and security to our throne." Then, looking again at the child: "And what a charming little page you've brought along with you today. I wish I had a boy like that. . . ." Then he asked the lad directly, "Who is your father, my boy? And where is your mother?"

The prince was flustered at these sudden questions and didn't know how to reply; but the king continued good-naturedly, "I'm just asking you who your father is, and where your mother might be. Can't you hear me, my lovely little lad?"

The boy looked questioningly at Chiken, who gave him a nod that meant "Yes, go ahead!"

"As to my father, he is the great king of this land of Magadha," began the prince. "My mother was called Lady Gosuiten, and was one of the thousand ladies who served the king. When my mother was carrying me, the other ladies envied her and tricked her into going to Mount Chikoshakuō, where she was killed. I was almost killed too, but the animals saved me and I lived with them in the mountains for three years. Then Master Chiken took me and educated me for four years at his temple. So now today, I can stand before the great king!" He had spoken his piece well.

The king was amazed and looked searchingly at the boy's face: indeed, he did look just like his father. "This must be my son. The child I thought was dead is alive! And grown so big!" The king wept for sheer joy. Then after a time he said, "I heard that Lady Gosuiten had vanished, but I never dreamed it was the work of my nine hundred and ninety-nine other wives. How dared they deceive me like that? I'll have their heads, every last one of them! Bring them here at once!" He was wild with fury.

"Your majesty," said the prince, "please calm yourself. The ladies went mad with envy and committed an evil deed, to be sure; but chopping off their heads now will not bring my mother back to life. Women are jealous by nature. That they would be consumed with envy of my mother, who could have a child while they could not, is not surprising. I don't think the nine hundred and ninety-nine ladies are especially wicked women, and I hope you will forgive them. For is it not said that we should return good for evil?"

It would have been only natural for the prince, whose mother had been murdered, to feel far greater hatred for the ladies than the king himself felt; and if the boy spoke as he did, it must have been because the profound teachings of the Buddha had deeply entered his heart. What could the king say in reply? He was filled with admiration at the boy's words.

"I understand what you say, but I can't leave matters like this. I'll drive them out of my kingdom!"

"Your majesty, there is just one thing I would like you to ask the ladies, and that is where my mother's head is. I want to find her skull and bury it together with the rest of her bones there on Mount Chikoshakuō. I'll build a tomb for her and perform the memorial rites there."

The king approved of this plan and at once summoned the nine hundred and ninety-nine ladies and pressed them for the details of their plot against Lady Gosuiten. The facts were known, and yet each of the ladies tried to defend her action and blame everything on the others. "*She* was the one who did it, you know. I had nothing to do with it at all," said one. "I was against it from the very beginning," claimed another. "Lady Gosuiten and I were very close," insisted a third. Listening to them, the king grew more and more disgusted; but when he asked the whereabouts of the Lady's skull, he received a frank reply: it was buried under the stable gate, about three feet down.

The king had the skull dug up and showed it to the prince, who wept bitterly. He took it to Mount Chikoshakuō, buried it in a tomb together with the other remains, and offered fervent prayers for his mother's salvation. He remained by her tomb night and day, seeking to console her spirit. Seeing this, the king said to him, "I understand how much you miss your dear mother. But you're becoming too preoccupied with her, now that she is dead. Didn't the Buddha teach us that all things are impermanent? If you understand that truth, can't you see that it's more important to care for your one remaining parent than for your mother, who has gone to the other world? I'd like you to stay with me in the palace from today on. I will make you crown prince."

It was a splendid offer, but the prince replied, "I was raised with grass and stones as bedding, not brocade cushions. I was raised surrounded by wolves and tigers, not by crowds of servants and ladies-in-waiting. My body still smells of the woodlands, and my heart is like that of wolves and tigers. How could a person like me live at court and take the lofty rank of crown prince? After I have prayed for my mother's soul, I want to return to the forests and mountains." Nothing the king could say had any effect; the prince sat beside his mother's tomb day after day, chanting the scriptures for the repose of her soul. Finally the king turned to Chiken: "The prince resents me. He thinks that it was I who killed his mother. I was a fool to believe the slanders of my nine hundred and ninety-nine wives. I never dreamed that the nine hundred and ninety-nine old women who burst into the Gosuiten Palace in the middle of the night had been assembled from all over the land and sent there by my wives. I didn't think they could be creatures of this world. I was afraid, and abandoned Lady Gosuiten. I was a coward, a coward and a fool!" The king wept.

Observing how repentant the king was, Chiken said, "Even the wisest of kings would think and act as you did. You were not at fault, and I am sure the prince does not resent you at all. Only, his feelings of longing for his mother are so strong. It would be easier to make the sun rise in the west than to change the prince's feelings."

The king grieved all the more. "Isn't there some way to make the sun rise in the west? Isn't there some way of freeing my son from his attachment to his poor dead mother and bringing him back to me?"

"There is a way, your majesty—one way only," said Chiken. "And that is to bring Lady Gosuiten back to life."

"Can such a thing be done?" asked the king.

"It can, through certain mystic rites and mantras. A monk who has undergone the strictest training can, once in a lifetime, bring the dead back to life by means of these secret rituals. I have studied the esoteric teachings and mastered the secret practices to a greater degree than any other monk. Through the power of my long years of study and practice, I will bring Lady Gosuiten back to life!"

Then Chiken set about erecting an altar on which he placed the skull and various other bones of Lady Gosuiten, exhumed from her tomb. For seven days and nights he prayed, taking neither food nor water. Then, something wondrous happened: on the last day, Lady Gosuiten suddenly appeared upon the altar. At that very moment,

Chiken, who had been praying continuously, fell down as if dead.

The king and the prince were amazed at the success of the ritual. "Mother, Mother, it's me, your son," cried the prince, clinging fast to Lady Gosuiten. "The son you fed with your milk for three years even after you died!" But the Lady had no memory of those three years. Strangely enough, she could remember all the happy things—how the king had favored her with his love, how she had borne a son; while all the bad memories—the nine hundred and ninety-nine other wives' abuse, the sudden appearance of the nine hundred and ninety-nine old women, the king's flight, her arrest by the seven soldiers, her beheading on Mount Chikoshakuō—all these had vanished without trace.

The king decided that Lady Gosuiten had such a pure heart that she had left all such bad memories in the other world, unwilling as she was to dwell on the evil in human beings. He wanted nothing more than that the three of them should live together happily for the rest of their lives. He knew, though, that the hearts of the people of Magadha had grown evil. Even if he drove the nine hundred and ninety-nine ladies from the court, there was no telling what kinds of plots they might hatch from outside. He could never trust the ministers, great nobles, and courtiers whom they controlled. And so he hit on the idea of going off somewhere, the three of them, with only a few loyal and pure-hearted retainers. He discussed the matter with Chiken, who advised, "Far, far to the northeast of this land of India, there is a country called Japan. In comparison with our Magadha, it is a very small island nation; but I have heard that it is green with trees, and that the hearts of the people are still pure. Why not go there?"

And so it was decided. But how would they go, you ask? In those days, there was a kind of boat that flew through the air—a boat equipped with wheels, for some reason. The king and his lady and the young prince got into this boat-with-wheels and flew high into the air, crossing many lands and seas. Several fine monks like Chiken himself also flew off in the direction of Japan in another one of these wheeled flying ships. And a select group of retainers also embarked on three more ships, racing through the air so as not to be left behind. All the ships arrived safely in Japan, in the mountains of Kumano, first at the Original Shrine, then at the New Shrine, and finally at Nachi. It was decided that the king would live at the first, Lady Gosuiten at the second, and the prince at the third site, and each became the lord of his or her particular mountain. The monks and retainers who accompanied them became the various gods and buddhas we know today. Thus, the gods who are known to us under names like "Prince So-and-so" were all originally retainers of the newly arrived royal family. And so you see, dear pilgrims, that these three mountains of Kumano are indeed holy places where the spirits of the prince and the king and the lady who crossed so many lands and seas are enshrined.

So come and worship at Kumano! If you do, you will receive rich blessings in this life, and in the life to come, rebirth in Amida's Paradise. Come to Kumano; yes, come to Kumano!

What's that? You say you have a question? You want to know what became of the nine hundred and ninety-nine ladies? Sorry, I forgot to tell you about them. They were very resentful at being left behind when the king flew off to Japan, so they had ships of their own made and went after him. There were ten ships in all, each holding a hundred ladies. Well, you can imagine the pushing and shoving. A good many of them fell off in mid-voyage, it seems. But most of the ladies did manage to make it all the way here to Kumano—oh, the tenacity of a woman scorned!

When the king saw them, he cried out, "I planned to create a new kingdom here in this fine land, and now you've come to spoil it all!" And he turned them all into "red worms." In this region, that's the term we use for a kind of big leech. We have lots of them in Kumano, and they're all transformations of the royal ladies who couldn't bear children.

When people go walking through the dark forests of Kumano, these "red worms" crawl unnoticed on to their bodies via their necks and wrists and ankles. They attach themselves firmly to people's flesh and then begin to suck their blood. It's said that they're especially fond of young men, and make quite a feast of them. At first it feels awfully good when they suck, but gradually it starts to hurt; and they're very difficult to pull off. There was a handsome young man (a famous actor from Kyoto, in fact), and the red worms got on him and sucked his blood. He laughed about it at first; but then, when he decided to pluck them off, he found he couldn't, and more and more of them attached themselves until at last he lay down and died there in the forests of Kumano.

It's a very holy place, Kumano is. You can meet your long-dead loved ones; you'll find a cure for grief and sadness; you can gain a long life, and a happy one. Only, be careful of the red worm. Come to Kumano; yes, come to Kumano! But do, oh do, be careful of the red worm.

Sanshō Dayū

山椒太夫

In the port of Naoi in the province of Echigo, there was a notorious slave-dealer named Yamaoka Dayū. He would offer lodging to travelers, luring them in with honeyed words, and then sell them to other slave-traders waiting in their boats just off shore. There were rumors of what was going on, and the local officials had issued orders forbidding anyone to give lodging to strangers, yet the evil practice was not easily uprooted. Yamaoka had made a small fortune in the trade. He was able to carry on because he was very cautious, taking care not to get caught; then, too, he made a point of bribing the officials and winning their goodwill.

One day a party of four including a mother and her two children came to Yamaoka's house asking for lodgings. The mother was a refined-looking woman of about thirty-five—probably the wife of a man of importance. With her were a daughter of about fifteen and a son who was perhaps two or three years younger. They were accompanied by a maid who looked to be about twenty. Yamaoka knew at a glance that they would be easy victims. The women were clearly unused to travel and innocent of the ways of the world. A kind word or two and they would be taken in. This foursome meant money: that thought alone was enough to make Yamaoka drool with excitement.

"You all look exhausted by your long journey and I'd like to offer you a room, but the governor has forbidden anyone to give lodging to strangers, so I'm afraid I can't."

"But why is it forbidden?" asked the lady.

"Well, there are slave-traders in this area from time to time, and they prey on travelers—especially women with children. There are some real scoundrels in this world, believe me."

"Are people as bad as that? I've never heard of such things happening in the village of Shinobu, where we come from . . ."

"Well, at any rate, be very careful. On the outskirts of town there's a bridge called Tsurumibashi (Coupling Bridge), and by it there's a woods that offers some shelter from the wind and rain. People around here say it's a good place for a traveler to stop for the night. I'm sorry, but I think you'd better spend the night by that bridge. I'm sure you'll find something better for the next night."

Yamaoka already had a plan in mind. He had planted the seeds of fear in the lady and ensured that she would stay by the Coupling Bridge rather than try going elsewhere. When night came, he would invite the little group, trembling with fear of wicked slave-traders, to stay with him. The next day he would take them by boat to his accomplices offshore and sell them.

When darkness fell over the northern port-town, Yamaoka went with a lantern to the woods beside the bridge. Though it was only mid-autumn, the northern night was cold, especially in this lonely woods at the edge of town.

He was sure the four travelers would be literally trembling with cold and fear; but, on the contrary, he found them all fast asleep.

"Excuse me, madam, excuse me—please get up. I'm sorry, but I forgot to tell you something very important earlier. Today is the fifteenth day of the eighth lunar month, Mid-autumn Night. Now, on this night when the moon shines brightly, they say a male dragon comes down from the sky, and a female dragon crawls up from the sea, and they have their yearly rendezvous here. That's why this bridge is called 'Coupling Bridge.' Anyway, after mating, the female gets very hungry and will gobble down anyone unlucky enough to be found nearby," concluded Yamaoka in a calm, cool manner.

The lady and her maid exchanged glances of horror at this news and now indeed began to tremble. "What a fearful thing! Oh, please, won't you let us stay with you, just for tonight?"

"I shouldn't, really. I may have trouble with the authorities later on . . . But never mind—I want to help you. You may stay in my house for tonight."

The lady and her maid could have danced for joy. They were sure they could rely on this stoutish man of forty. As in the old saying, they had "met a buddha in the midst of hell." People who are suddenly plunged into a terrifying situation tend to regard anyone who says a kind word to them as a buddha in the flesh.

When they reached Yamaoka's house, his wife went over and whispered in her husband's ear: "Well, you've brought along another bunch of dupes, I see. But I've had enough of this slave-trading business. You never know when the authorities'll figure everything out; and if they do, I'll be branded a slave-trader's wife. No, if you must carry on with this business, give me a divorce first!"

"This isn't slave-trading, it's helping your fellow-man! I felt sorry for the lady and her children, with all their troubles, so I decided to let them stay—that's all! I gave them a room out of sheer goodness, like the merciful Kannon himself."

"Oh, really?" said his wife, and went over to the two women. "My husband says he's putting you up out of the goodness of his heart—'Buddha Yamaoka,' I guess we should call him! Well, stay as long as you like. But if by chance he suggests that you go off somewhere with him, you be sure and let me know."

Now the lady thought it a bit odd the way this woman was talking; but perhaps it was the custom of the people of Naoi to say things like this. At any rate, she was not greatly concerned. Watching all this, Yamaoka decided that at this rate his wife would be saying something she oughtn't to the lady. Besides, "make haste to do good" was his motto, so he went right up to his guest and said, "You seem to be in something of a hurry, dear lady. Now, the fastest route to Kyoto is from this port by boat to Tsuruga, and I've just learned that there's a boat leaving before dawn tomorrow. Of course, we'd be happy to have you stay on here for some time, but if you *are* in a hurry, may I suggest tomorrow's boat?" The lady nodded in reply.

Well before dawn, Yamaoka secretly led the little group from his house to a waiting boat. The night sea had an eerie look to it. Particularly to these people who had never seen the sea, a trip by boat seemed fraught with danger. Nevertheless, the two women had great confidence in this "buddha met in hell." He rowed the boat a short distance out to where two more boats were moored in the offing. The two waiting boatmen drew Yamaoka's boat close to theirs and whispered something in his ear. They seemed to be counting something on their fingers and having quite a lively discussion. It appeared that the transaction was successfully concluded, for Yamaoka turned to the group in his boat: "These two boatmen are my nephews, and each of them wants to take you to Tsuruga. They're being awfully stubborn about it. I'd like to ask you a favor, so that neither of them will lose face: would you and your maid go in one boat, and the little master and mistress in the other? You'll all be heading for Tsuruga, after all."

The lady agreed to this suggestion, so she and her maid got into the front boat while the children boarded the second.

"Well, then, I'll be on my way. These two are excellent boatmen, so just leave everything to them. Take good care of yourselves, and have a nice safe journey to Kyoto!" And he rowed back to shore.

The two boats proceeded together for a while, but then the second boat began to fall behind. The lady begged the boatman, "Please row more slowly. The children's boat is getting further and further away from us." But the boatman just grinned and answered, "Never mind. You'll be together again at the next port. Just relax and enjoy the view of the sea on this fine morning." But the second boat not only drew no closer but actually moved off in the opposite direction until it could hardly be seen. "What's the meaning of this, boatman? It's going in the wrong direction!"

The immediate reply was loud laughter. Then, "You finally noticed, eh? Yamaoka sold you! Each of us paid five *kan* for the four of you. The two little mites are on their way now to be sold off somewhere or other."

And so the lady understood that she had been duped. "You tricked us! You plan to sell us all, don't you? If I'm to be sold into slavery, I want to be with my children! That would make it bearable. But to be separated like this—it's too cruel! My poor Anju, my poor little Zushiō!"

She got up on the stern and shouted in a loud voice in

the direction of the other boat, now a mere speck in the far distance. "Anju! Zushiō! Forgive your mother for being too trusting. Forgive me! You're going to be sold as slaves, but never lose heart! Anju, don't lose the holy image of Jizō you have around your neck—he'll save you in time of danger. And Zushiō, guard the paper with our family's lineage on it. Put up with every difficulty that comes, and show that paper to one of the Ministers or Grand Councilors. Someday your father's name will be cleared, our lands restored, and the sun will shine on you both again!" She shouted as loud as she could, but her voice could hardly reach the other boat. She and her maid took one another's hands and broke down in tears.

"It's tough, of course," said the boatman. "But it's your own damn fault, after all. You're a foolish, ignorant woman— that's why it happened. Try looking at it that way! Anyhow, I need to make some money out of this. I guess I can sell this little parcel here to a whorehouse. She should bring maybe ten *kan*. And you, I'll take as my wife. I'm still a bachelor, and now at last I've found me a good bride. What's the saying? 'All things come to them that wait'?"

At these words, the maid went at the boatman: "This lady as your wife? Unforgivable impudence! This lady is the wife of a provincial governor in charge of fifty-four counties around Shinobu. I won't let you lay a finger on her!"

"She may be the wife of a provincial governor in charge of fifty-four counties, but in this boat she's just another woman. There's only the three of us now, and I can do what I like with both of you, 'cause I'm lord and master here! A lord with a beautiful wife *and* a concubine. Maybe I should start things off with the concubine. . . ." The boatman decided to have a little fun pretending to chase the maid, who tried hard to escape. As they struggled, she slipped and fell into the sea. She couldn't swim, and disappeared into the waves as they watched. "Uwataki, Uwataki," cried the lady, but it was no use. "Uwataki's dead! She's dead, and I don't want to go on living either!" She tried to jump into the water, but the boatman held her back.

"Damn! I got too randy and lost myself a valuable piece of property. Should've waited till we got to shore. Damn! If I let something happen to you, I'll lose five whole *kan*. You'll be my wife, or be sold for a whore, but the one thing you *won't* do is die on me!" He tied her hands and feet with thick rope and put her in the bottom of the boat.

Anju and Zushiō, after being separated from their mother, were taken to the distant port of Yura in the province of Tango where they were bought by a man named Sanshō Dayū for thirteen *kan*. There were great differences of opinion as to the right price for the girl and boy. They were obviously children of good family, and it would enhance anyone's prestige to have such well-bred slaves—that was the positive view. The negative view was that they would be worthless as laborers. Thus, their price fluctuated wildly. They had been bought and sold twenty times over by the time they reached Yura, and it took quite an effort for Sanshō to convince himself to lay out thirteen *kan* for the pair. He was known in the area for his wealth and was engaged in a variety of businesses including fishing and the making of salt. He had five sons named, in numerical order, Tarō, Jirō, Saburō, Shirō, and Gorō. Having made a fortune for himself, he had now begun to be concerned about the future of his descendants. He planned on each of these two slaves eventually marrying and producing offspring, who would in turn serve Sanshō's children and grandchildren as slaves, and so on forever. It was a piece of luck, then, that their hometown was Shinobu in the faraway province of Mutsu; for, lacking relatives, they would have no one to rely on but their new master.

Summoning them, he began, "I hear you two are from Shinobu, but what are your names?"

"We are from the village of Shinobu in Date County. We left our home on the eighteenth day of the third month together with our mother; but at Naoi port in Echigo, we were tricked by a wicked man who took us from our mother and sold us to slave-traders. We have no particular names, master, so please call us whatever you like."

The truth was that Anju did not want these fellows to call her and her brother by their real names.

Sanshō replied as if in the best of moods: "Country bumpkins like you two could hardly be expected to have proper names, I suppose. Anyway, I'll give you some nice ones. You, girl, can be 'Shinobu' (endurance), after your village. And your brother we'll call 'Wasuregusa' (grass of forgetfulness). Be sure you forget everything else and just devote yourself to my service! From tomorrow on, Shinobu will go to the seashore and draw water from the sea. Wasuregusa will cut firewood—three shoulder-pole-loads a day. Around four tomorrow morning, give the boy a sickle and shoulder-pole and the girl a bucket and ladle."

Early next morning, Zushiō took his sickle and shoulder-pole and went to the mountains, while Anju went to the seashore with her bucket and ladle. At home, they had been surrounded by servants and had never themselves held anything heavier than chopsticks and a rice bowl. Even so, Zushiō did his best to cut firewood with his sickle. But the wood was too hard, and he could hardly cut one piece, much less three shoulder-loads. As he worked away, the sickle-blade broke and he cut his fingers badly. The boy wept with chagrin. Then he thought of his sister, who must be enduring the same sort of hardships. "It doesn't matter about me, but my poor, poor sister! How can she draw water from the sea, in the cold and with the winds and the waves? I bet she's already lost her bucket and ladle to the waves by now." He broke down and wept, not so much for himself as for his sister. Just then some mountain-folk came by and asked him why he was crying. When the boy told them the reason, they exclaimed, "Poor little lad! He must be from a good family, and this mountain work is too much for him." Then they quickly cut some brushwood and bound it into three shoulder-loads for him.

Anju too, though she went as ordered to the seashore, kept floundering in the high waves and was not able to fill her bucket at all. She was at her wits' end and, doubly grieved at the thought of what Zushiō must be enduring in the mountains, wept bitter tears. Some diving-women came by and saw her. "It's too much to ask a young lady like her to draw water from the sea," they said, and did it for her.

When evening came, Zushiō returned with three shoulder-loads of firewood and Anju with her quota of sea-water. "Just look at the firewood this brat has cut!" exclaimed Saburō, Sanshō's third son. "He said he'd never done it before, but this is a perfect job—the ends are all nice and even. It's an expert's work. Since you're so good at it, brat, you'd better bring back ten loads tomorrow, not just three!"

Then he issued orders to the sea-folk and mountain-folk not to help the new slave-children cut brushwood or draw water, under threat of dire punishment. The local people, seeing the order, thought Saburō a cruel devil of a man, but what could they do? The next morning the sister and brother went to work as on the day before, but this time the sea-folk and mountain-folk passed them by: "We'd really like to help you, but it's forbidden by order of that cruel Saburō."

Zushiō was in despair and thought there was nothing for him to do but die. But if he had to die, he wanted to die together with his sister; and so he went to the seashore. Anju too had been thinking that the only solution for her was death, so she greeted her brother joyfully. The two of them filled their sleeves with pebbles and, taking each other by the hand, climbed up on to a large rock. "Look on me as the mother you were parted from at Naoi in Echigo, and I will look on you as the father who was exiled to Anraku-ji in Tsukushi," Anju said. Each gazed at the other as if seeing his mother or her father. They were about to leap from the rock together when suddenly they heard a loud voice from below.

"Don't die—you mustn't! You have a mother and father. Think how they'll grieve if they hear of your deaths. If you live, there'll surely come a day when you'll see your dear parents again."

Startled, they looked down and saw "Kohagi from Ise," a girl about five years older than Anju who was, like them, a slave of Sanshō Dayūs. She climbed quickly on to the rock and, putting an arm around each of them, pulled them back to safety and sat them down.

"You may think you are the two unhappiest people in the world, but you know, there are people much worse off than you—and I'm one of them. I was raised in Uda, in Yamato province, and though our family was not as well off as yours, we had everything we needed. But my mother died, and my step-mother came. She tricked me and sold me to a slave-dealer, and that's how I came to be here. You're still children, but I'm not, and I've experienced every kind of abuse a woman can be put through. In my misery, I decided to put a mark on this staff every time I was sold, and now there are forty-two marks. In these last five years, I've tasted every suffering there is and endured every humiliation. But I'm still alive, and I've become a stronger woman because of it all. Now there's no suffering I can't bear, and no humiliation I can't endure. In fact, I've learned to find a joy in bearing everything. So, compared to the pains and humiliations I've suffered, yours are very light. In a sense, you were too blessed before, too fortunate. Your earlier happiness makes what you have to go through now all the harder to bear. But I'll teach you how to cut firewood and draw water. And, what's more, I'll teach you how to deal with Sanshō Dayū and Master Saburō. You can look on me as an older sister. This older sister may not be able to do much, but at least she's learned a lot about putting up with troubles and humiliations. I want to help you learn how to endure your fate." Kohagi wept as she spoke, seeing in the two children an image of herself five years earlier, when she'd known nothing of the trials of life. Remembering herself back then, she wept and resolved to protect these two little ones as much as she could. Anju and Zushiō rejoiced at this unexpected appearance of an "elder sister," and the three of them hugged one another happily.

The children were still not very good at their tasks of cutting brushwood and drawing water; but, thanks to Kohagi's cleverness, they were able to get through each day without incurring the wrath of Sanshō Dayū and Saburō. At last, New Year's Eve came round. Sanshō Dayū called his son to him and said, "I can't stand the sour looks of those two. Just looking at their gloomy mugs puts me off my food. It's New Year's, and lots of people will be coming to offer good wishes: the god of good fortune should be coming along too! But one look at those two, and our guests will start feeling gloomy themselves, and the god of good fortune will up and run away. So send them off somewhere."

"It's just as you say, Father. Shall I pack them off to the usual place?"

"Yes, why not?" said Sanshō Dayū.

"The usual place" was a hut beside one of the side gates to their residence. It was an old-fashioned taboo-hut, where women who were thought to be impure due to childbirth or menstruation were kept apart from everyone else. Sanshō Dayū used it as a kind of prison for slaves who had committed a fault of some sort. But what a shock it was to this young, innocent pair to be made to spend the festive New Year season in such a place of defilement! The previous New Year's they were living comfortably in a large mansion in Shinobu (though without their father), enjoying games of backgammon and battledore-and-shuttlecock. How different their present state was! More than the cold and the hunger, the children found the humiliation hard to bear. Finally, Anju said to her brother, "You should run away, Zushiō. Get away from here as soon as possible and go to the capital."

"How can I run away? It's impossible."

"If you go down the other side of the mountain where you cut firewood, there's a road that leads straight to the capital, they say. You *should* run away. You mustn't stay on in a place like this forever."

"You're the one who should run away, Anju. Or, why don't we run away together?"

"It'd be dangerous for the two of us to try it. What one can do, sometimes two cannot. I'd be a drag on you in all sorts of ways, being a woman. Besides, a woman can't restore the fortunes of our family. You must show the paper you have to the Court in Kyoto. And when you succeed in the world, please come back for me."

This debate as to who should be the one to run way was overheard by none other than Saburō, who happened to be passing by the taboo-hut at the time. "Those two brats are planning to run off somewhere," he reported to his father, who at once ordered them brought before him: "What's this talk I hear about you two running away?" he said in a fury. "How dare you, after I've been so good to you? You're returning evil for good, you are! I paid thirteen *kan* for you, and you've worked off a thousandth of that at best. And yet you plan to run off. Well, I won't have it! I'll put my mark on your faces so everyone'll know you're my slaves for good, and there'll be no more talk of running away. Get everything ready, Saburō."

Saburō made a fire and heated a branding-iron with the "Yama" mark on it. Then he grabbed Anju by her long hair and wound it around his fist: "How about it, Shinobu? I'm going to brand that pretty little cheek of yours to show you belong to Sanshō Dayū!"

"No, no, you mustn't!" cried Zushiō. "If you brand my sister on her face, it'll be your loss too. Now you can be proud of having such a beautiful slave, but if you brand her, you'll ruin everything. So leave her alone, and put two brands on my face instead!"

But the merciless Saburō applied the hot brand to Anju's left cheek. Zushiō was so terrified at the sight that he tried to run away, but Saburō caught him by the hand. "You're just a brat, for all your fine words. Let's put our brand on your cheek too!"

"Please don't do that to Zushiō," cried Anju. "It'd be terrible for the family heir to have a mark on his face. A scar on the forehead might mean he'd fought with honor, but this kind of scar is pure shame. I don't care if you brand me again, but leave Zushiō alone, please!"

"No. Both of you need branding," Saburō said roughly as he applied the "Yama" branding-iron to the terrified little boy's left cheek. Nearby there was a hollowed-out pine-tree trunk that was used as a bathtub. Saburō turned it over and shoved the two children under it, giving orders that no food be given them—that they be left to starve.

Anju and Zushiō, cooped up in their crude little prison, no longer had the energy even to speak; they simply clung to one another and wept bitterly. Late that night, however, they had a secret visitor—Kohagi. She had smuggled some food in to give them: "I couldn't do anything to help you today, and now look what's happened! Forgive me. This food is from master Jirō, Sanshō Dayū's second son. He feels sorry for you and saved his own dinner for me to give you. So, here: *this* is from him, and *this* is from me."

The food Kohagi brought was of a sort the children were never given to eat: sea-bream sashimi, boiled shrimps, and the like. And it had hardly been touched.

"Master Jirō left all this for us? . . ." They felt grateful for his kindness.

"There *are* good people in this world," said Kohagi. "You sometimes find a buddha right in among the devils. So you mustn't despair. I'll keep sneaking in food for you from Master Jirō, and from me too." Having made this promise, she left.

The New Year's festivities were well over when, on the sixteenth of the First Month, Sanshō Dayū called Saburō to him: "They're probably dead by now, but go check to make sure." When he got to the pine-tree bathtub, Saburō found that, though they looked ill, with muddy complexions, the children were still alive. Surprised, he reported back to his father.

"Somebody was probably feeding them on the sly," said Sanshō. "But never mind. Since they're still alive, set them to work tomorrow morning." So Saburō ordered the children to start drawing water and cutting firewood again beginning the next day.

But Anju spoke up: "Master Saburō, I have a request. Zushiō is still too weak to work on his own. Please send me to the mountain along with him." For once Saburō gave her a smile as he answered, "All right. You can go to the mountain too." Anju was very happy; but then suddenly he grabbed her by the hair: "If you're going to the mountain, we'll have to make a man of you. You don't need this long woman's hair—cut it off. No, wait—I'll do it for you." And he roughly cut off Anju's hair with his dirk. Poor Anju stood there with her crudely cropped head while Saburō's attendants burst out laughing. "Look at this monster here! The head's male, the body's female, and it's even got a brandmark burned into its face, like some horse or ox. It's a monster, a real monster!" said one of them, doing an imitation of a monster. The onlookers burst into even louder laughter then.

And so the brother and sister went off to the mountain, followed by the mocking laughter of Saburō and his cronies. They did not stop at the place where Zushiō usually cut brushwood, though, but went on to the very top of the mountain, where they sat down on a rock. Anju took the image of the Bodhisattva Jizō from around her neck and addressed it: "You're supposed to be our guardian, dear Jizō, and yet you haven't helped us at all. You didn't do a thing when we were sold into slavery and when our faces were branded. Do you think you deserve to be called our guardian? If you really are our guardian saint, please take better care of us from now on!" She bowed to the image and had Zushiō do the same. When they had finished paying reverence to Jizō, they glanced at one another, and then both cried out at the same time: "The mark on your face—it's gone!" Truly, the bodhisattva had worked a miracle for them, no doubt feeling that not to do so now would be to fail completely in his role as guardian saint.

When she saw that the terrible mark was gone from her brother's cheek, Anju said, "This is a sign from Jizō that you should run away. Go down the other side of the mountain, then find a village, and go to the temple. Hurry!" She took the holy image and placed it around Zushiō's neck.

"But what about you? . . ." Zushiō hesitated, worrying

about what terrible things Sanshō might do to Anju if she stayed behind.

"You don't have to worry about me. They'd never kill a woman," she said with a laugh. When she saw Zushiō was still hesitant, she started to walk briskly back the way they had come.

"All right then, I'll go. I'll go to the capital. But come back up here for a moment so we can say goodbye before I go."

Anju came back, and brother and sister shared a parting cup. Of course there was no saké, and no cup either; but they scooped up water from a mountain stream with a cup made from the leaf of a dwarf-bamboo, and shared that. Then Anju gave her brother a pat on the shoulder and sent him off: "So this is goodbye for now." Zushiō, his resistance overcome by his sister's firmness, moved off reluctantly down the other side of the mountain. Anju watched until he disappeared from view and then cut some brushwood for form's sake and started back. When she arrived at Sanshō's house, he at once demanded to know what had happened to Wasuregusa.

"We got separated when we were cutting brushwood on the mountain. I'm sure he'll be coming back soon on his own."

"You're lying. I can tell from the look on your face. You've helped him to run away." Sanshō angrily ordered Saburō to punish her.

"You're asking for it, you little bitch," Saburō said with a cruel smile. He tortured her with fire and then with water. Anju broke down and wept from the pain, but Saburō just tortured her the more. "Look at you, you're crying! They say there's five kinds of tears—tears of sadness, tears of rage, tears of resentment, tears of happiness, and crocodile tears. I bet you're crying from happiness at having helped

Wasuregusa get away. Or maybe they're crocodile tears that you think'll get you off lightly. But it won't work! Now talk! Where did he go?"

"I'll talk, I'll talk. Please stop, please!"

"So you're going to talk, eh? You stubborn bitch."

When the torture stopped, Anju said, "I'm sure he'll be right back. When you see him, tell him his sister died without saying anything."

Saburō became even more enraged at these words and applied still more painful tortures to the girl. "What the hell is this, bitch? You don't answer my questions, and say whatever you feel like?" Finally the pain grew unbearable, and Anju stopped breathing.

"Stubborn bitch!" said Sanshō Dayū. "We took such good care of her to make sure she'd talk, and then she dies on us. A weakling, for all her big talk! Anyway, Wasuregusa can't have gotten far. Let's go after him." So, leaving Anju's body where it lay, he and his followers went in pursuit of the boy.

Zushiō had done just as his sister had told him: he went down the mountain to a nearby village and sought help at the local temple. It was an old temple called Kokubun-ji, which is now in ruins; but at the time there was a priest living there. When Zushiō broke in on his solitude, he was performing a sacred fire ritual.

"I'm being pursued by Sanshō Dayū. Please help me."

The priest was aware of Sanshō's reputation for greed and cruelty and quickly guessed what had happened. He took an old leather basket from a closet and put the little boy inside. Then he tied it with many cords, from top to bottom and side to side, put a net around it, and hung it from one of the roof beams. Having done all this, he resumed the fire ritual as if nothing had interrupted him. Soon there was the sound of loud voices, and Sanshō Dayū's party rushed into the room.

"Hey, priest, did a servant come in here just now?" demanded Saburō.

"What? You say you want a service said? Well, I'm always pleased to say a service for the pious—and I do so appreciate the luncheon people give me afterwards! There haven't been many good luncheons lately, and I'm quite famished. Yes, I'd be delighted to say a service."

"Not a *service*, you old fool! I'm asking if a *slave* has gotten in here!"

"Oh my, yes! When the wind blows, the leaves just pour into the chapel. And not just leaves—I get lizards and snakes and foxes and badgers. I really don't know what to do!"

"Not *leaves*, you old shit—a *boy-slave!*"

With this, Saburō ordered his followers to search the whole temple. They searched the sanctuary, the priest's living quarters, and his private altar, and then under the veranda, behind the ceiling, and below the floor-boards; but they found nothing.

"That's strange," said Saburō. "We can't find the boy, but he certainly came in at the gate, and there's no sign of him escaping from the back. He's got to be here somewhere. This shit-priest is hiding him, that's for sure. Now talk! If you don't, you'll be sorry." Saburō suggested to his father that the old priest be *made* to talk, but that far even Sanshō Dayū was unwilling to go: "I agree that he's probably hiding the boy, but I won't have him tortured. He's under the protection of the Buddha, after all. Now, I'm not a believer or anything, but I don't like the idea of roughing up someone in the Buddha's service. There might be a curse of some sort. So, Saburō, we'll have to call it a day. We can always come back later."

The search-party was about to leave when Saburō stopped them. "No, Father, it's a bit too early to go home. I've been looking at the ceiling for the past few minutes, and I see that that leather basket hanging from the beam there is swaying even though there's no wind. And the net around it looks new. I'm sure this bastard has hidden the boy in that basket. If we go back without checking that, we'll regret it forever." He started to pull at the net. His elder brother Tarō, unable to hold back any longer, went up to him. "Hold on a minute, Saburō. There are lots of old images and scriptures in these ancient temples, and they often put things of that sort that are no longer of use in baskets like this, tie them with cords, and hang them from the roof beams. If the cord looks new, maybe it's because the priest just hung it up today or yesterday. And you know, sometimes in these mountain temples even when there's no wind outside, there's a draft inside due to the shape of the valleys. Anyway, the house of Sanshō Dayū is not so poor that the absence of just one servant will make such a difference."

Tarō was the eldest son and heir but seldom took an active role in matters. He had always disliked his father's and younger brother's greedy and cruel ways; but being a good-natured sort, he didn't like to stir up trouble. Now he was speaking in what was, for him, a very decisive manner. But Saburō answered, "I'm willing to listen to you in some matters, Elder Brother, but not in this. It'd be like having your prey right in front of you and then letting the beast escape! Even the Buddha isn't always merciful." He swiftly grabbed hold of the net and lowered the basket. He was too impatient to untie the cords so he cut them all with several slashes of his sword. But when he removed the lid, something extraordinary happened. The image of Jizō that Zushiō wore around his neck gave forth a golden flash like lightning that sent Saburō sprawling below the veranda.

"Well, what did I tell you, Saburō? You should regard yourself as lucky that the Buddha spared your life!" said Tarō. At any rate, there was nothing Sanshō Dayū could do but take his leave, saying to the priest as he did so, "Sorry to have disturbed your reverence. We'll be on our way for now, but we'll be back, you can be sure of that."

The priest had been on pins and needles earlier, wondering when Zushiō would be discovered. He was concerned because he felt sure that discovery would mean death for the boy; and he was even more worried about what kind of punishment would be meted out to him in that case. But now the holy bodhisattva Jizō had worked a miracle and saved not only Zushiō but the reverend priest as well!

When the search-party had disappeared into the distance, he helped the lad out of the basket. The two joined hands, rejoicing at their delivery and thanking the Buddha from their hearts for his mercy. Zushiō declared that he would go to the capital the very next day and then come back as soon as possible for his sister. The priest, amazed at the boy's innocence, warned, "You must have been very tenderly raised, my boy. You're too naive, much too naive. Sanshō Dayū gave up for today, but you can be sure that he's keeping watch on the two of us. One word that you have left this temple, and your pursuers will be after you just three to five miles down the road. No, I've started something, and I've got to finish it. I'll take you to the capital myself."

And so the priest put the boy back into the basket, tied it up with cords from top to bottom and side to side, and set off for the capital carrying the basket on his back. If he met anyone on the way and they asked him what he had on his back, he always answered, "I am a priest of the Kokubun-ji in Tango, and I have an ancient image known as 'the Branded Jizō' in my temple. But it's in such bad condition that I've decided to take it up to the capital to have it repainted."

And so the priest traveled from Tango to Seventh Avenue in the western part of the capital, where there was a chapel to the god of Suzaku. Here he released Zushiō from the basket and then said farewell. The boy had made it to the capital safely, but now he had no idea what to do in this city he had never seen before. The language of the capital was very different from his own, and no one would believe him when he announced himself to be the son of the Governor of Shinobu. He was in a great quandary, when he heard someone say that the Shitennō-ji in Naniwa (a temple founded by the holy Prince Shōtoku) was famous for its miracles. If one offered prayers for something there, they were bound to be granted. And so he decided to go to Shitennō-ji. While he was there, a procession went by led by a famous wonder-working priest known as Ajari Daishi. As he passed, Ajari Daishi noticed Zushiō and, pausing for a moment, instructed the lad to enter his service as a page. Zushiō, not knowing what else to do with himself, meekly obeyed.

Now just at this time, a certain Grand Councilor, known as Umezu-no-in because he lived in Umezu to the west of the capital, had a strange dream. He was childless and had long wanted to adopt a suitable boy. In his dream, Prince Shōtoku appeared and said to him, "Go to Shitennō-ji and worship me. On your way home, I will provide you with a fine son." And in the dream, the Prince gave the Grand Councilor a handsome young boy.

Umezu-no-in decided to go at once on pilgrimage to Shōtoku's tomb at Shitennō-ji and then to pay a visit to Ajari Daishi, with whom he had been on cordial terms for a long time. The holy man was surrounded by a great crowd of attendant youths and boys; but as the Councilor glanced at them, he was struck by one boy in particular who looked exactly like the lad in his dream. "This is the very child Prince Shōtoku promised me!" he thought joyfully. "Ajari Daishi, please give me this page as my adopted son." Of course the holy man was surprised, as were the other priests and youths and boys in attendance: why would the Councilor suddenly choose to adopt this boy sitting unobtrusively in one of the last places? Nevertheless, the request was honored; and afterward, when the lad had been properly bathed and groomed, they saw that he radiated a beauty and elegance surpassing that of any son of a Minister or great nobleman.

So it was that Umezu-no-in joyfully took Zushiō back with him to the capital, where he prepared to introduce his newly adopted son to all his friends. These Great Ministers, noblemen, and courtiers were very impressed by Zushiō's handsome appearance, but the general opinion was that "it would not do to take a person of doubtful origin as adopted son of a Grand Councilor." Learning of this, Zushiō took out the lineage chart he always carried and placed it before one of the Great Ministers. The Minister opened it and read what was written: "Zushiō-maru, heir to Fujiwara Masauji, Magistrate of Iwaki, Lord of the fifty-four counties in Mutsu."

"Is he, then, the heir to the famous Fujiwara Masauji, Lord of Mutsu? Lord Masauji was falsely accused and exiled to Tsukushi, but now he has been pardoned and will soon return to the capital. A wonderful turn of events! And Umezu-no-in has found himself a fine son, truly a treasure of a son!" This was what everyone said, congratulating the Grand Councilor and envying him his good fortune.

Word of all this soon came to the ear of the Emperor, who commanded that Masauji should pass the headship of the family on to Zushiō, who would henceforth hold the fifty-four counties in Mutsu and, in addition, the Anraku-ji region, where his father had been exiled, as a special holding "to provide sustenance for his horses."

Zushiō responded, "I have no need for the lands at

Anraku-ji in Tsukushi, or even for the fifty-four counties in Mutsu. I ask, rather, that Your Majesty grant me the area around Yura in the province of Tango."

The Emperor felt all the greater goodwill toward Zushiō on account of his lack of greed. "Well then, since it is your earnest request, We shall give you Yura in Tango in place of Anraku-ji in Tsukushi, as sustenance for your horses. As for the fifty-four counties in Mutsu, you shall hold them, whether you wish to or not."

Now Zushiō was eager to leave for Tango as soon as possible and be reunited with his sister. Anju must be enduring great hardships, he thought. If Zushiō had hoped to rise in the world, it was only in order to save Anju and then look together for their mother. A decree was issued in the new governor's name, saying that on such-and-such a day he would proceed to Tango and lodge at the Kokubun-ji.

Great was the surprise of the resident priest at the Kokubun-ji: "Though the land of Tango is small, still there are many famous temples. And yet the new governor wishes to stay in this neglected place! There must be something behind it. I'm not aware of doing anything especially wicked; but, after all, no one's perfect—'Beat anything, and dust will rise,' as the saying goes. It's a dangerous situation. Perhaps I'd better run away. . . ." And so he did, as swiftly as he could.

Thus, when the new governor of Tango arrived at the Kokubun-ji, the priest was not there to greet him. Zushiō ordered that a thorough search of the province be made, and at last the priest was found and brought before him. The old man was trembling with terror, but the governor approached him respectfully: "Thank you, reverend sir. You saved my life."

"I never saved your life, Lord Governor," wailed the old priest. "Please execute me quickly and get it over with!"

"Look at my face carefully. I am the boy you hid in the leather basket."

"I've heard of ugly ducklings turning into swans, but this is amazing! What a change in less than half a year!" cried the priest, rejoicing to see Zushiō again. "I never dreamed that that lad would become governor of the province."

"Do you know what's become of Anju, whom I had to leave behind at Sanshō Dayū's?" asked the governor.

"It's a very painful thing to say, but your sister died at the hands of Sanshō Dayū and his son Saburō. I managed to obtain her body for cremation. Here are her ashes and her hair," the priest concluded, showing him a small packet of remains.

"I decided to go to the capital and make my way in the world because I wanted to be able to save her," Zushiō said, sobbing and pressing the remains to his face. "But she's dead, and my success means nothing."

The next day, Zushiō summoned Sanshō Dayū, who announced to his five sons: "We're being told to appear before the new governor himself! He probably wants to ask about the famous places and old ruins in this area. If we give good replies, he may reward us with some land. If he *does* ask what land we want, be sure to request as much as possible! The more we get, the better it'll be for our descendants."

When Sanshō Dayū appeared before Zushiō, the new governor smiled warmly and inquired about the region, its famous places and historical sites. Sanshō had each of his five sons answer in turn, reporting amusingly, and accurately, on the various places to be seen.

"Well now, I'd like to give you all some land; but would you prefer something fairly large or something rather small?" inquired the governor.

Bull's eye! thought Sanshō, smiling to himself as he made sure that his sons asked for "something fairly large." But just as Sanshō and his sons were congratulating themselves on their success, the new governor said something rather odd. "Oh, by the way, there used to be a couple of children, sister and brother, named Shinobu and Wasuregusa at your place. How are they? Are they still all right?"

Startled, Sanshō answered, "Yes, well, I bought that pair last year for thirteen *kan*, but they were of no use at all—we didn't know what to do with them. Still, we took good care of them and let them do pretty much as they liked. But that ungrateful Wasuregusa, the younger brother, up and ran away. Worthless rascal, returning evil for good like that! Then the older sister, Shinobu, fell into the ocean and drowned one day when she was supposed to be drawing water."

"I see," said the governor. "That Wasuregusa was a worthless rascal, was he?"

"He most certainly was, Your Excellency. Why, I paid thirteen whole *kan* for him, and he ran away without doing even a thousandth-part of the work he owed me. A real good-for-nothing, he was."

"I see. . . . A real good-for-nothing? Well, that good-for-nothing is here before you now: I am that worthless rascal Wasuregusa! I am, in fact, Zushiō, son and heir of Fujiwara Masauji, Magistrate of Iwaki, Lord of the fifty-four counties in Mutsu. I was sold to a slave-dealer at the port of Naoi and then bought by you, Sanshō Dayū—you, who took such good care of me. Not three shoulder-loads of brushwood, but ten a day, you told me. And you shut me and my sister up in that hut by the side gate at New Year's, and taught us the taste of hunger. And you branded this face with your 'Yama' mark—I'll never forget the pain! And then you tried to kill us, in the pine-tree bathtub. And you, Saburō, chopped off my sister's long black hair with your dirk. And then, finally, the two of you tortured and killed her because she helped me to escape. She died rather than say anything that might help you—isn't that true? Oh, I miss her so! She was a wonderful sister. It was due to her that I've come into my own. . . . But her sufferings were much, much worse than mine. And you were responsible for those sufferings. I might be able to forgive what you did to me, but what you did to my sister, never! If crimes like that could be forgiven, this would be a world without gods or buddhas. And it's not only for my sister. Who knows how many people have died at your hands? How many people went to their deaths cursing you both? I can hear the voices of all those you murdered, my sister and all the others; their bitter, angry voices.

"Saburō, you asked for 'a fairly large piece of land,' and you shall have it. Hades is much larger than this land, and filled with the torments of many hells, so they say. You can look forward to the pains you will suffer there."

I cannot bring myself to write in detail about the punishment that Zushiō imposed on Sanshō Dayū. The merciful Mori Ōgai in his version of the story lets the villain go unpunished. (Surgeon-General of the Imperial Army though he was, had he forgotten the severity of the code of military justice?) But that was not the way things happened. If the people of that time had had a chance to read Ōgai's novel, their reaction surely would have been along the following lines: "Don't be ridiculous! Sanshō Dayū and Saburō must receive retribution for their crimes. And for such terribly cruel acts, the punishment too needs to be a little cruel." Therefore, though I do not wish to describe it in detail, let me simply relate the bare facts: Sanshō Dayū was condemned to "death by sawing," in which the criminal was buried in earth up to his neck, and then his head was sawed off. They took Sanshō Dayū to the very spot where Anju had been killed and buried him in the prescribed manner; then Saburō was made to do the sawing. After his father was killed, Saburō himself was buried alive, and his retainers, who had taken part in Anju's murder, were ordered to saw off *his* head. They say that during his father's execution Saburō said, "According to the teachings of the holy saint Hōnen, even the greatest evil-doer can go to Paradise if he recites the Name of Amida Buddha. You can recite the Holy Name even now, Father, with just your head sticking out of the earth. Recite the *nembutsu*, then, and let the sound of this saw against your flesh and bones be like the sound of gongs and wooden drums in a temple liturgy. I'll be coming soon, so wait for me at the entrance to the underworld, Father. I'll carry you across the River of Hades on my back."

And so the matter was ended. Tarō entered the priesthood, as he had long wished to do, and spent his days in prayer for the repose of the souls of his father and brother as well as Anju and other dead slaves. Jirō inherited his father's manor-lands—or rather, the half that was not confiscated.

Thus, the evil were punished and the good rewarded.

Zushiō went to the capital and was reunited with his father. He received permission from Umezu-no-in to leave his household and then returned to the village of Shinobu together with his father, the priest of the Kokubun-ji, and Kohagi, to become Lord of the fifty-four counties in Mutsu, now restored to his family. And so our story comes to a happy ending.

There is, however, an interesting and well-known sequel. After returning to Shinobu, there was still a person Zushiō had to find: it was, of course, his mother. People said she was in Ezogashima, the northernmost "Island of the Ezo People," present-day Hokkaido. It would be impossible to find her in such a place, everyone said, but Zushiō would not give up and went all the way to that northern isle to search for her. He had already been there for one month; but, far from finding his mother, he had not even had any news of her.

Then one day he saw a strange sight. A woman somewhat past her middle years was chasing birds with a long pole—or rather, she was pretending to chase them. She was a "bird-catcher," a kind of wandering entertainer of that time. (Zushiō had heard that some of these "bird-catchers" served as prostitutes as well.) This particular woman was, sadly, blind in both eyes. She pretended to pursue birds with her long pole, saying all the while, "My dear Zushiō, where can he be? My dear Anju, where can she be? My dear Uwataki, where can she be?" Then she fell to the ground.

When he heard the names Zushiō, Anju, and Uwataki, Zushiō felt a kind of charge run through his body. Could this be his mother? He listened once more, carefully. Again, the woman made as if to catch a bird, saying "My dear Zushiō, where can he be? My dear Anju, where can she be? My dear Uwataki, where can she be?"; and again she fell down. Yes, it was his mother! Zushiō ran to her and embraced her. "Mother, I'm Zushiō! Zushiō, who was parted from you at the port of Naoi!"

But this unfortunate blind woman answered: "I don't know who you are, sir, but please don't make fun of a poor old woman. What I'd like from you is a penny." Zushiō felt so sad he couldn't keep back his tears.

"Please listen to me, Mother. I really am Zushiō, your only son. After we parted, I was sold to a slave-trader and ended up serving a fellow called Sanshō Dayū, in Tango. But I escaped and went to Kyoto, as you said I should. I met a Great Minister and explained everything that had happened; and the fifty-four counties in Mutsu were restored to our family. I was able to rise in the world thanks to the holy